**"Hope you don't mind getting dirty,"
Vaughn said as the cabdriver drove them
to the restaurant. His thigh was inches
from hers and he could feel himself getting
further and further turned on by this
woman and they hadn't even touched yet.**

"I don't mind," Miranda said. "In fact, the dirtier the
better. Though I do wish I'd opted to change clothes."
She looked down at her attire.

"Why?" Vaughn asked, glancing in her direction. "You
look beautiful."

"But a bit overdressed for the beach, right?" She laughed.

He smiled. "A bit. That's what makes you so adorable."
He reached across the short distance between them and
tucked a wayward strand of hair that had fallen in her
face behind her ear. When she looked up at him, her
eyes were filled with desire. Vaughn wanted to sweep his
mouth across hers and taste her, but the car came to a
stop.

"We're here!" she said brightly.

Yes, we are, Vaughn thought. If the car hadn't come to
a halt, it was a certainty he would have acted on the
rampant desire he felt for Miranda.

Dear Reader,

His San Diego Sweetheart is an exciting new book in the Millionaire Moguls series featuring three heroes: Vaughn Ellicott, Jordan Jace and Christopher Marland. Vaughn is a former navy man turned sexy surfer with a billion-dollar surfing business. He has no time for love because he never received it growing up as a child, but that doesn't stop him from risking his heart when he offers Miranda Jensen a marriage of convenience to save her inheritance.

Heightening the drama is a delicious sabotage subplot in the Millionaire Moguls organization. To find out who's the saboteur, pick up the next installment in the series: *Seduced in San Diego* by Reese Ryan.

I enjoyed researching San Diego and learning about surfing. With my adventurous streak, I may even try it one day.

For more info, visit my website, www.yahrahstjohn.com, to download my latest ebooks or write me at yahrah@yahrahstjohn.com.

Best,

Yahrah St. John

HIS
SAN DIEGO
Sweetheart

Yahrah St. John

Special thanks and acknowledgment are given to Yahrah St. John for her contribution to the Millionaire Moguls miniseries.

Recycling programs
for this product may
not exist in your area.

ISBN-13: 978-1-335-21659-5

His San Diego Sweetheart

Copyright © 2018 by Harlequin Books S.A.

For questions and comments about the quality of this book please contact us at CustomerService@Harlequin.com.

Printed in U.S.A.

Yahrah St. John is the author of twenty-seven books. When she's not at home crafting one of her sexy romances with compelling heroes and feisty heroines with a dash of family drama, she can be found in the kitchen cooking one of her gourmet meals discovered on the Food Network for her husband. Or this thrill-seeking junkie can be found traveling the globe seeking out her new adventure. A graduate of Hyde Park Career Academy, she earned a bachelor of arts degree in English from Northwestern University. St. John is a member of Romance Writers of America, but is an avid reader of all genres. She lives in sunny Orlando, the City Beautiful, where there's great weather all year round. For more information, please visit www.yahrahstjohn.com.

Books by Yahrah St. John

Harlequin Kimani Romance

Two to Tango
Need You Now
Lost Without You
Formula for Passion
Delicious Destiny
A Chance with You
Heat Wave of Desire
Cappuccino Kisses
Taming Her Tycoon
Miami After Hours
Taming Her Billionaire
His San Diego Sweetheart

Visit the Author Profile page
at Harlequin.com for more titles.

Acknowledgments

To my newest right hand, Christy Massie.
Thank you for the encouragement and morale boost!

Chapter 1

Vaughn Ellicott, Jr. sliced through the crashing surf at San Diego's Black Beach on his custom-made surfboard. Surfing was his own piece of heaven and gave Vaughn the freedom he desperately craved after the rigors of Navy life as a lieutenant. For a decade, he'd done as he was instructed because that was what his father, Commander Vaughn Ellicott, Sr., expected of him. But now, Vaughn did what he wanted to do and surfing was as natural to him as breathing, even though at six foot two, he towered over some of the other surfers. When he was in the water, he felt an inner peace with Mother Nature as he challenged himself on the waves. He saw the waves as opportunities to lose himself and find himself at the same time.

And he had found himself. Five years ago, he'd started a company, Elite. After he began designing his own wet suits, other surfers had begun showing interest in his work. Seeing a business opportunity, he'd formed Elite and sold his wet suits online. From there, sales had skyrocketed. His high-end scuba gear company now sold dive computers and any other gear a surfer needed, from surfboards and bags, to leashes and wax. The fact that his business interests mirrored his passion was perfect for Vaughn.

Even though it was nearly the weekend, it was long past time for him to depart the beach. Vaughn should have left thirty minutes ago. He was due to attend a meeting of Prescott George—the Millionaire Moguls club, as the press liked to dub them. The nickname had been given to them because their national organization was comprised mainly of millionaires. The club had been formed in the 1940s by Prescott Owens and George Rollins. Today, Prescott George's numbers had grown into the thousands and there were chapters all over the world. Vaughn was proud to be a member and the treasurer of the San Diego chapter.

Emerging from the Pacific Ocean carrying his surfboard, Vaughn began peeling off his wet suit when a pair of feminine eyes caught his gaze. She was giving him the once-over. And he didn't mind the attention; he was used to it. In social circles, he was a sought-after millionaire bachelor with an impressive seaside estate. And on the beach, he was looked up to because of his fearlessness and passion for the sport.

Vaughn had no trouble attracting women. *Any* kind of woman. So much so that he couldn't get a moment's peace. Women adored his physique which he spent a great deal of time honing, and his impressive assets, but Vaughn had yet to find one worth keeping around. They all seemed a little too eager to be with a Millionaire Mogul, and so he dealt with them with a long-handled spoon, engaging only when he wanted companionship or needed physical release.

Vaughn gave the beautiful stranger one final intense stare. Long silky dark hair. Expressive almond-shaped eyes. Tawny brown skin slightly kissed from the sun. Although she was wearing a sleeveless dress, it was a bit too formal and didn't fit with the unusually warm spring afternoon. Her only admission that she knew she was at the beach was the fact that she'd kicked off her pumps and they lay partially submerged in the sand. Maybe that was why she stood out.

But there was something sad about her though. And as much as Vaughn would love to find out her story, he was late. He purposefully trudged through the sand toward the locker room so he could get changed into business attire. Today was important for the San Diego chapter. Today, the Moguls had visitors. Joshua DeLong and Daniel Cobb, co-presidents of the national chapter in Miami, were in town.

There were rumors that San Diego could be awarded Chapter of the Year. Vaughn certainly hoped that was the case; it would be a prestigious honor. The chapter had been successful in attracting younger members to the organization, but it hadn't come without drama. Some of the older members of Prescott George were less enthused. They felt like they were being pushed out to make room for a younger, hipper generation, which simply wasn't true. Vaughn believed in the Moguls motto: *From generation to generation, lifting each other up.* If they didn't pull in the next generation, how could they possibly continue providing college scholarships to needy students and funding to inner-city organizations?

All of these thoughts coursed through Vaughn's mind as he took a quick shower, changed into a designer black suit with pinstriped tie and headed for his Ferrari California T in the parking lot. He smiled when he saw the expensive sports vehicle with its turbocharged engine and drop top. For such a new company, Elite had done quite well in the marketplace and afforded Vaughn the luxury of a fancy car, private jet and a beachside mansion in La Jolla. Before turning on the engine, he glanced back at the beach, wondering why a woman as beautiful as that stranger looked so forlorn. He shrugged. Wasn't his problem. He had bigger fish to fry. He turned the ignition, the Ferrari roared to life and Vaughn sped away.

The San Diego Prescott George chapter was located inside a historic brewery near the East Village. Vaughn parked outside the renovated, environmentally friendly building and strode inside. He walked through the offices, glancing around at the exposed brick, loft ceilings and state-of-the-art canopy lighting that made up the Moguls club as he headed to the all-glass conference room. As in other Prescott George offices, pictures of their founding members, Prescott Owens and George Rollins, hung on the walls, reminding them of who started the organization. The meeting was already underway and multiple sets of eyes glowered at Vaughn as he made his way near the head of the table where Christopher Marland, the chapter's president, sat next to two strangers who Vaughn could only assume were Daniel Cobb and Joshua DeLong.

Vaughn gave a halfhearted smile as he sat down. "Sorry. I was unavoidably detained."

"By what? A wave?" Another member guffawed.

Several other members at the table chuckled softly at the joke, but they immediately stopped when Vaughn glared at them.

"You might want to wipe off the evidence," Christopher concurred as he reached across the table and brushed sand off Vaughn's shoulder.

Darn! He thought he'd caught it all. It wasn't easy changing into a suit at a beach locker room. Perhaps he should endow the county with a new state-of-the art facility to ensure something like this didn't happen again?

"Getting back to business," Christopher said, returning his focus to the meeting. "We're pleased that the chapter is being graced with such an honor."

"So, it's true?" Vaughn interrupted him. "We're Chapter of the Year?"

"That's right," one of his Miami brethren replied. He was tall and fair-skinned with striking blue eyes. Vaughn didn't know brothers could have eyes that color. "We feel that San Diego has shown not only the vision, but the gravitas necessary to propel Prescott George into the future."

"Daniel Cobb." The other gentleman reached across

the table to shake Vaughn's hand. "And that's Joshua De-Long." He inclined his head to the fair-skinned man beside him. "We know it couldn't have been easy. There had to be opposition to change, probably as much as we've encountered in Miami."

"You mean when you ousted a Rollins?" an older member asked from the far side of the table.

"No!" Daniel responded hotly. "Ashton realized it was in the best interest of Prescott George to have some new blood with fresh ideas at the helm. He's still very much involved in the Miami chapter."

"I doubt that," the man muttered underneath his breath.

"If you have something to say," Joshua DeLong responded, "by all means, speak up. We welcome feedback. Good or bad."

Daniel grabbed Joshua's arm and whispered something in his ear.

Vaughn couldn't resist smiling. He liked Joshua DeLong. He was his kind of guy. Just look at his appearance. He wasn't wearing the customary suit like the rest of the members of Prescott George, Daniel included. He wore trousers and a T-shirt with a blazer he'd probably haphazardly thrown on at the last minute to show he was making an effort. Vaughn understood wanting to dance to the beat of your own drum. It was what he'd been doing for years now that he was no longer an officer in the United States Navy.

The older member remained mum.

"Good then," Daniel said. "Then, if it's alright with you—" he turned to Christopher "—we'd like to announce your selection as Chapter of the Year at your annual benefit in a few months."

"Sounds like a mighty fine idea," Vaughn chimed in. "It would be great press for the organization and chapter. Don'tcha think?" He glanced around the table at the other members.

"My skills at handling the press are fully at your disposal," Joshua DeLong said.

"Skills?" Another member laughed. "Infamy is more like it." Several other members expressed their amusement.

Vaughn stepped in. "It's those very same tweets, Instagram posts and Snapchats that have helped connect us with new members."

"You mean the young whippersnappers who can't be bothered to be here?" The older man glanced around the room.

"They aren't on the board," Christopher responded tightly and Vaughn noticed the firm line across his mouth. "That's why they have mentors to groom them into becoming leaders. It doesn't happen overnight."

"I'd love to hear more about this mentorship program," Daniel responded. "Do you both have time to discuss after the meeting?" He directed his question to Christopher and Vaughn.

"Absolutely," they both said in unison.

The chapter meeting concluded soon after and Vaughn watched the other members shuffle out of the room. Once the room had cleared, Joshua spoke first. "Looks like you face the same resistance to change that we've encountered in Miami."

"We do." Christopher nodded.

"How do you combat it?" Daniel inquired.

Vaughn chuckled, but Christopher responded. "Clearly, we haven't squashed it entirely. We've just had to push forward with our agenda."

"Attracting younger members?" Joshua offered. "Talk to me about this mentorship program."

"Let's retire to the lounge for cigars." Christopher gestured for the men to walk ahead of him.

The lounge housed several large chocolate leather sofas surrounded by modern and edgy furnishings. The men sat in a semicircle and discussed the future of Prescott George. Christopher offered their guests expensive cigars which another member had brought back from Cuba. Eventually, conversation returned to San Diego's progress with millennials.

"We've had some great events like beachside barbecues, art gallery openings and wine tastings, specifically geared to a select group of young millionaires," Christopher said. "We have a great artist in our midst, Jordan Jace. You may have heard of him?"

Joshua nodded. "I have his work. It's cutting-edge."

"Jace is like a lot of our younger members. They like being part of an organization in a limited capacity," Christopher responded. "Of course, I know our small-time events are a far cry from the charity galas you have in Miami."

"Hey, that's how you have to roll in South Beach," Joshua replied with a chuckle as he leaned back and puffed on a cigar. "Go big or go home."

"Our chapter does plenty of good work. We just do it in a less traditional format," Christopher intervened and Vaughn couldn't help but notice how uptight the man always was. But that was Christopher; he certainly wasn't Vaughn's favorite person after he'd dumped his baby sister Eliza all those years ago. Vaughn didn't think she'd ever truly recovered. He suspected it was why she'd moved to New York, to have a fresh start and get over Christopher. She was back now and keeping a low profile.

Hours later, after they'd shaken hands with their Miami brethren and given them their best advice, Christopher returned to his office to work on an architectural project, but Vaughn was restless. He hadn't had nearly enough time at the beach today. He'd gone into Elite's office early that morning and taken care of some pressing business and hadn't been able to get out to the beach until the late morning. Then, he'd had to cut his surfing time in half because of the Prescott George meeting. He needed to breathe in some fresh, salty ocean air. Hopping into his Ferrari, Vaughn headed back to his second home, the beach.

Miranda Jensen sucked in several deep breaths. She was glad the surf god who had majestically surfaced from the Pacific Ocean wearing a snug-fitting wet suit was gone. She colored when she thought about how she'd stared so openly at the magnificent specimen of a man. Unabashedly, she'd watched him glide the zipper of his wet suit down as he'd shaken off the excess water. He had a sculpted torso which had revealed hard, defining muscles underneath and eight, yes, eight-pack abs that were impossible to ignore.

The man was ripped!

His chest had been surprisingly smooth and hair-free and Miranda would have loved to flick her tongue across the brown discs of his nipples.

Sweet Jesus!

What was wrong with her?

She'd struggled to gulp in air as he'd walked straight toward her, never taking his eyes off her. At first, she'd thought he was going to make a pass at her. There was obvious interest lurking in those penetrating dark depths. He'd seen her giving him the eye, but instead of talking to her, he'd kept moving, leaving Miranda to wonder if it was because of her man curse. She was still hypersensitive when it came to men these days. *How could she not be?* She had a bad track record when it came to the opposite sex and the broken heart to prove it.

Since her breakup with Jake, whom she'd thought was the love of her life, Miranda had had a series of unsuccessful relationships. Jake had unceremoniously kicked her to the curb in a favor of a promising career in Japan with a pretty something coworker he'd met abroad. Her rebound guy, Anthony, was a womanizer and notorious cheat. She'd caught him in bed with one of her supposed friends. The last joker, Chris, she'd dated had only been after her money, ingratiating himself into her family in the hopes he'd hit the jackpot. Thankfully, she'd gotten hip to his real agenda before she'd married him; otherwise it would have been a disaster of epic proportions.

And now all Miranda could hear was the sound of a clock ticking in her head.

No, it wasn't her biological clock.

It was the timer on her fortune, which was about to slip through her fingers if she couldn't find a groom. She had her grandfather to thank for putting her in the predicament she was in. He'd passed away a couple of months ago and as a condition of his will, he required that his only grandchild, Miranda, marry by the age of thirty or forfeit her inheritance altogether. If she didn't marry, the huge sum of money that was rightfully hers would go to one of her grandfather's charities and forever vanquish Miranda's dream of opening her own upscale bed-and-breakfast by the ocean. Or at least postpone it.

Fury boiled inside Miranda's veins.

She valued her independence, but perversely she needed to be tied to a man in order to achieve her personal goals.

But this time love would have nothing to do with it.

Miranda didn't know if she'd been trying too hard to find Mr. Right. Or whether she was just one of those people who were destined to be alone. Nevertheless, the rejections and lies of her former lovers had hardened her heart. She'd vowed that no man would ever hurt her again. If they were after her money, so be it.

But it would be on *her* terms.

She'd taken a leave of absence from her job as a hotel administrator in Chicago to go husband shopping. She was hoping to find a man and make him an offer he couldn't refuse: a marriage of convenience with a huge cash payday.

After her Adonis had come out of the sea, Miranda had left the beach and gone to a nearby café for a cool beverage. It was casually chic and she hoped offered a good drink. It wasn't like she'd been dressed for the beach anyway. Her lace sheath dress was definitely not beach attire and as for her pumps, she was still trying to get the sand out of them.

"Can I get you another drink?" the bartender inquired. "It's happy hour now and cocktails are half priced." When she didn't answer quickly, the bartender walked away to help another customer.

Miranda glanced down at the pomegranate martini she'd been nursing since she arrived. She'd only been in San Diego for twenty-four hours. Her best friend, Sasha Charles, had picked her up from the airport last night and deposited her at her hotel. Sasha had offered Miranda to stay at her place, but Miranda had been adamant that she didn't want to put her friend out. That wasn't the real reason. She didn't want to share her real plans with Sasha because she knew Sasha wouldn't approve. And so she'd opted to stay at a hotel instead. It was an elegantly appointed hotel that would suffice for what she hoped was a short stay.

Miranda was hoping that she could find Mr. Right quickly enough that she would meet the one-month deadline looming over her head, before her inheritance was given away. Her parents, Tucker and Leigh, were just as upset as she was by her grandfather's stipulation. She'd been hoping to find a loophole, but her attorneys had been unsuccessful. And now desperate times called for desperate measures.

She was just about to order another martini when the

surf god from this morning came strolling into the café. He sat down at the far end of the bar away from her and talked to the bartender. Given the easy rapport they shared, they must know each other.

She allowed herself a few minutes to adjust to seeing him fully dressed. But this time, he was no less potent than he'd been on the beach earlier. In fact, she'd say he was more so. Her devastatingly sexy stranger had closely cropped black hair, an angular face that held bushy eyebrows and facial hair that was more than a five-o'clock shadow, but not a full beard, and the dreamiest eyes she'd ever seen. He was dressed in distressed jeans that clung to a gloriously tight behind, from what Miranda recalled, and a graphic T-shirt that hugged his defined biceps. Miranda couldn't forget how delectable his body had looked earlier and licked her lips in remembrance.

Why was she having such a reaction to this man?

He clearly didn't have a nine-to-five job. Why else would he have been at the beach when most people were at work? And here he was again, which told her that he could be exactly the sort of man who could be compelled by the promise of a hefty cash payout.

Decision made, she slid off the bar stool with as much modesty as she could in a dress, grasped her purse dangling from the stool and moved toward her mysterious stranger. What was the worst he could do? Brush her off? He'd done that earlier and she was no worse for the wear.

"Ahem." Miranda coughed loudly, bringing her right hand to her mouth.

He glanced up from his conversation, but didn't make any effort to speak. Instead his dark eyes gleamed like glassy volcanic rock as he boldly raked her from the top of her hair to her now aching feet. Pumps were definitely not made for all the walking she'd done today. "Are you done with your appraisal?" Miranda inquired. Flirting could work to her benefit if it garnered his interest. Though he would soon find out she had an agenda.

"Nearly." He continued to scan her critically for several more moments before he beamed his approval and looked her dead in the eye.

"And?"

A perplexed look crossed his features. "And what?"

"Do you like what you see?" Miranda inquired.

"Yes. Yes, I do very much."

Miranda's insides jangled with excitement as she slid onto the bar stool beside him. The bartender came to her immediately. "Have you decided if you'd like another?"

"Actually, I'd like something stronger." She turned to her companion. "What would you recommend?"

He grinned a delicious, stomach-curling smile. "Max, get her a bourbon, same as me." He swiveled around to face her. "It's a bit strong, but I think you'll like it."

"I like strong," Miranda countered. "Men, that is."

"Is that a fact?"

She smiled coquettishly. "It is indeed. I noticed you earlier surfing." She inclined her head toward the beach that was about a hundred yards away.

"And did *you* like what you saw?"

She raised a brow. He'd seen her watching him, so she answered honestly. "You know I did. It was quite entertaining watching you out there."

"And afterward?"

An image of him in the wet suit flashed across Miranda's mind. "The view wasn't bad either."

Her stranger laughed heartily and Miranda liked the sound of it. It was deep and masculine and the very air around her seemed electrified being next to him.

"Well, aren't you a breath of fresh air. You actually say what's on your mind."

"Miranda." She extended her hand. "Miranda Jensen."

"Vic Elliott." His grip was strong and his hands were massive, swallowing her small ones in his. "Pleasure to meet you, Miranda. And here's your drink." He motioned to the bar where the bartender had placed her drink along with another bourbon for him. He held up his glass and she did the same. "Cheers."

He tapped his glass against hers and watched her take a sip. His gaze was so compelling that Miranda had to focus on sipping her drink. It was as strong as he said it would be, but she needed liquid courage. "I like it."

"A lady after my own heart."

"And would there be any other ladies of your heart?" she inquired. Better she know now what she was up against than waste her time with a man who wasn't available.

He gave her a sideward glance. "There's no one special."

"How about some dinner?" Miranda inquired. "Since I'm new to San Diego, you choose."

"Would love to."

Vaughn liked Miranda Jensen. She was open and direct. He appreciated her honesty. She knew what she wanted and wasn't afraid to put all her cards on the table. He liked that she'd approached him in the café. She seemed unconcerned about what he did for a living or how much money he made. Twice today, she'd seen him, first at the beach and now at the café. She probably thought he was a drifter she could have a one-night stand with while on a business trip to San Diego. And that was just fine with him. She was a fine-looking woman and he wouldn't mind getting better acquainted with her. In or out of bed.

After they finished their bourbons, Vaughn decided to take Miranda to a local seafood spot that had the best crab claws in town. Rather than drive his Ferrari and call out the fact that he was loaded, Vaughn opted for an Uber. When he was getting to know a woman and to weed out gold diggers only interested in his money, he usually gave minimal details about himself, including the name Vic Elliott. In the Navy, his men had nicknamed him Vic and it stuck, so Vaughn used it along with an abbreviated version of his last name.

"Hope you don't mind getting dirty?" Vaughn said as the Uber driver drove them to the restaurant. His thigh was inches from hers and he could feel himself getting further and further turned on by this woman and they hadn't even touched yet.

"I don't mind," Miranda said. "In fact, the dirtier the better. Though I do wish I'd opted to change clothes." She glanced down at her attire.

"Why?" Vaughn asked, glancing in her direction. "You look beautiful."

"But a bit overdressed for the beach, right?" She laughed.

He smiled. "A bit—that's what makes you so adorable." He reached across the short distance between them and tucked a wayward strand of hair that had fallen in her face behind her ear. When she glanced up at him, her eyes were filled with desire. Vaughn wanted to sweep his mouth across hers and taste her, but the car came to a stop.

"We're here!" she said brightly.

Yes, we are, Vaughn thought. If the car hadn't come to a halt, it was a certainty he would have acted on the rampant desire he felt for Miranda.

He'd been about to kiss her; Miranda was absolutely sure of that fact. The way he'd looked at her with those searing dark eyes that seemed to read into her soul told her so. And she would have let him. Hadn't her heart been hammering in her chest, just sitting beside him, thigh to thigh, shoulder to shoulder? Even though they'd only known each other barely an hour. She would have let this handsome and sexy stranger have his way with her.

What would that have been like? Would his kiss have been soft and sweet? Or hard and hungry?

She needed to get control of herself.

She wasn't here for romantic entanglements. She needed a husband—and quick. This man looked like he wasn't desperate for money, but wouldn't mind some extra cash in the bank. And it didn't hurt that he wasn't bad on the eyes either. Not that her marriage would be a real one. She had no intentions of consummating the marriage. They would only stay together long enough to ensure her inheritance before going their separate ways. But first, she had to ask him.

After exiting the car, Vic led her inside the seafood restaurant with his hand lightly resting on the small of her back as he propelled her forward. It was in no way untoward, but Miranda felt it all the same. He kept it there until they were seated and he'd scooted her chair underneath her before taking his own.

"You're quite the gentleman."

He grinned. "My mama taught me how to treat a lady."

"Sounds like she's a wise woman," Miranda offered.

"She's an amazing woman." The way he said it told Miranda that he was close with his mother. A man who had a good relationship with his mama was always a good sign.

After the waiter filled their water glasses and took their drink orders, Vic immediately begin firing questions at her. "So where are you from, Miranda?"

"Chicago."

"And what do you do there?"

"I work in the hotel industry," she responded.

"And what brings you to the West Coast?"

"I have a pressing business matter that I've put off for far too long and now it requires my attention."

He laughed and shrugged off her evasiveness. "That's rather vague, but you don't have to share. I understand the need for anonymity."

"And what is it that you do?" Miranda inquired. If he was going to put her on the hot seat, why shouldn't she return the favor?

"I used to be in the Navy, but now I surf."

"Why the Navy?"

"If you couldn't tell, I love the ocean and the sea. Quite frankly I've never felt at home anywhere else except on the water. It's a part of me."

"I've a laundry list of places I'd love to go to, but I imagined you've traveled the world extensively while in the Navy."

"It did afford me certain luxuries, but we usually weren't there long enough to truly take in the culture. Now Chicago, on the other hand, I'd steer clear of. I can't imagine living in the Midwest and having to deal with all that cold and snow. How do you do it?"

Miranda shrugged. "I suppose you get used to it. Have you always lived in California?"

Vic nodded. "It's close to the ocean, just how I like it."

The waiter returned with their drinks and they continued happily chatting about Vic's travels until dinner came. Miranda was a good sport when the waiter put bibs on both her and Vic so their clothes wouldn't get soiled. A platter of succulent crab claws with mustard sauce and Lyonnaise potatoes were placed in front of them.

"You have to try this." Vic reached for a crab claw and after dipping it in the mustard concoction, he leaned over the table and fed it to Miranda. Her eyes grew large at the romantic gesture and she toyed with the idea of not accepting, but in the end, she grasped Vic's large hand in hers and bit into the crab, taking a large chunk into her mouth.

Vic sat back in his chair, but his eyes never lost hers

as a sigh of ecstasy escaped her lips at the sweetness of the crab meat and tanginess of the mustard sauce. Desire zinged through her and Miranda knew a blush had to be tinting her cheeks.

"That's delicious…"

"I know, right?" The tone of his vice was jovial, but the look on Vic's face was anything but. It was a hungry look. A look that told Miranda she'd awakened the beast. She watched him place a small heap of potatoes on her plate. And thank God for it. Miranda was completely tongue-tied. She'd known she was attracted to Vic. And it scared her. If she chose this man—there was no way theirs would be a marriage of convenience.

Chapter 2

"I had a lovely evening," Miranda said when Vic insisted on seeing her back to the hotel and walking her to her room. She knew what he was up to. He wanted to get in her pants and as much as that scenario would ease the sexual tension that had been flying between them throughout the night, it wouldn't solve her current situation.

Vic was a viable candidate for a husband, but she couldn't let her hormones run away with her, despite how much she wanted to. And boy, did she want this man something fierce. She'd love to have free and unfettered access to roam her hands up and down his chiseled body, to relish him taking her to new heights, because her intuition told her Vic knew how to please a woman in the bedroom. All that patience waiting for the perfect wave. There was no way he was a slam-bam-thank-you-ma'am kind of man. He'd take his time exploring every sensual side of her nature.

They walked in silence after exiting the elevator. Neither of them too keen on talking. Even though they'd done just that for hours. They'd actually shut down the restaurant, only leaving when it closed. Miranda had thoroughly enjoyed her evening with Vic much more than she would have guessed when she slid off her bar stool at the beachside café and introduced herself.

And now they were here.

At her door.

Miranda took an extraordinary amount of time fumbling to find the hotel card, but when she did, she didn't use it. Instead, she spun around to face Vic. He'd moved closer to her during that short time and now he was a breath away from her, a tantalizing breath.

"Vic…"

He pulled her into his arms and she was surprised when she didn't object. Instead, she allowed him to come closer and mold his body to hers until every inch of their lower bodies were touching. Then his head lowered until his forehead was touching hers. Miranda's breath caught in her chest.

God, how she wished she was one of those women who could bed a man and walk away the next day, but she wasn't. Furthermore, her situation didn't allow her to have a weak moment and have a night of passion with Vic. She had to think with a clear head and *not* with other body parts.

"Ask me in," Vic whispered huskily. "You know you want to."

He was right.

She did.

She wanted him desperately, but tomorrow morning she'd be in the same boat she'd been in yesterday. Or maybe even worse. Vic was dangerous. He was the kind of man she could fall for, lose her head over when practicality was needed here.

"I should go inside." She pushed against his rock-hard chest and Vic released her.

"If that's what you want."

She didn't dare look up at him, because he'd know it was a lie. So Miranda kept her head low and murmured, "Yes, it is." Then she quickly used the card to let herself in the hotel room and immediately closed the door.

But not before she caught a glimpse of Vic's stunned expression and his last words. "I'll call you."

* * *

Did Miranda really just close the door in his face?
Vaughn stood staring at her hotel door in stunned disbelief. *Was he losing his touch?*

He'd felt her heat when he'd pressed her against him. Her body had reacted to his, instantly molding itself against his. She'd wanted him too, but for some damn reason she was denying herself—hell, the both of them—a night of mind-blowing sex. Because that was exactly what she would have had in store. He'd been nursing an erection on and off for half the night and that was just from a brush of his hand across her back, accidental foot play underneath the table or a look from Miranda from across the table. If he'd had all night with her, she wouldn't have slept. He would have made sure to explore every inch of her body from head to toe.

But alas, he wasn't getting that chance.

She'd closed the door, and if he wasn't mistaken, locked it.

Was she locking it to keep herself from opening it or from letting him in?

Shaking his head, Vaughn headed to the elevators. He just couldn't understand how he'd gotten his signals crossed. And what possessed him to say he'd call her? Maybe he should leave well enough alone and move on to greener pastures.

The elevator doors chimed and opened. Vaughn stepped inside.

As the doors closed, Vaughn knew he wouldn't move on. Miranda Jensen had intrigued him and not many women did. And it wasn't just the chase that had turned him on; he wanted to know more about her. Throughout the night, he realized they'd talked more about general topics than they had anything personal. Miranda had been cagey about revealing any personal details other than her name and job title, which made Vaughn's antenna come on high alert. She may not be interested in his wealth, but she was certainly hiding something.

And Vaughn wanted to know what it was.

But more importantly, he wanted Miranda. And he would have her.

There was no trace of Vic Elliott. He didn't exist.

After returning from the amazing dinner she'd shared with the man, Miranda had decided to Google him. Find out more about this mysterious stranger who had captured her attention since emerging from the sea. But she couldn't find a single thing about him. There wasn't a record of Vic anywhere online. She'd tried several spellings of his name, including using Victor, and still her results had been fruitless.

He'd lied to her about something as fundamental as who he was.

How could she have been so blind yet again?

Was she destined to be a loser when it came to picking the right man? It stung because Miranda was sure she'd seen something in Vic that was special, something that she'd never encountered before with the other men she'd dated. Over drinks and dinner, they'd shared true companionship, laughing and talking about a number of topics from sports to politics to religion. Though she was woefully out of her league when it came to sports. Instead, Vic hadn't made her feel dumb or stupid and they'd even discussed catching a game.

Now she knew he'd been lying the entire time.

But had she been that open? No. But at least she'd given him her real name. If he wanted to find out more just as she was researching him, he could. *If* he was interested, but he couldn't have been if he'd lied to her. He was probably married and had given her a fake name in the hopes she'd spend the night with him. And her traitorous body had wanted to. Oh how she wanted to indulge in all the desires of the flesh. His sinful flesh.

His hard, lean body had been made for a woman's touch. Of that, Miranda was sure.

Except she wouldn't be partaking because Vic, whatever his name, wasn't hers. She sighed. It had been nice to wonder *what if*, if only for a little while.

The next morning, Vaughn was up with the birds. Images of the raven-haired beauty from the beach had dominated his dreams, causing him to toss and turn in his king-size bed. Eventually, he'd thrown back the covers and, after brushing his teeth and showering, donned an Elite wet suit and gone to the beach. He dove into the waves. Whenever he needed to clear his mind, surfing was a good cure-all. He could lose himself in the powerful forces of Mother Nature and forget whatever it was that ailed him such as a certain body part which ached to be released.

Vaughn couldn't remember the last time he'd had an erection that had gone unsatisfied. Usually, when he was with a female, the night would come to its inevitable conclusion, him in the arms of a beautiful woman.

Not last night.

Miranda Jensen had rebuffed his advances, sending him home with a hard-on like some love-struck teenager. And it irked him. Not because she'd turned him down, which, although rare, could happen. He was rankled because he knew Miranda wanted him equally as much as he wanted her, but instead she'd made them both miserable by pushing him away. The question was why?

There had to be more to the story and he would find out.

Several hours later after returning home to shower, Vaughn drove to his office. Elite's headquarters were located a few blocks away from La Jolla Shore's beach. Most of his staff wore shorts, T-shirts and sneakers because Vaughn wanted a laid-back vibe at the office and found it made for productive workers. They appreciated not only the dress code, but the free healthy snacks catered by a local food truck, the coffee bar as well as a game and nap room onsite. He treated his employees well and consequently had their loyalty.

He greeted his assistant, Kindra, as he stopped by her desk. Kindra was one of the sweetest girls he'd ever met. She had a wholesome, all-American quality to her five-foot-five, blonde appearance. She was athletically built, wore no makeup and rarely had he seen her in anything other than a skirt, but she was the best help he'd ever found.

"I'm surprised to see you here," Kindra said. "I'd have thought with today's forecast you'd be catching some waves."

Vaughn grinned. She knew him so well. "I already did."

"So you thought you'd come in and do a little work?"

"If that's okay with you?" He gave her a wink.

She shrugged. "You're the boss." Kindra followed him inside his office and caught him up to date on what he'd missed that morning. Once he was up to speed, Vaughn dismissed her so he could open his laptop and satisfy his curiosity.

He typed Miranda Jensen into his browser and searched.

He was shocked by what came up.

Miranda was no gold digger on the hunt for her latest meal. She was a wealthy heiress from a prominent Chicago family. He went on to read how her grandfather had made a killing in the finance world and as his sole granddaughter, she was due to inherit millions.

Vaughn leaned back in his chair and rubbed his beard. So he hadn't been the only one not being completely truthful. Although she'd shared that she was from the Windy City, Miranda hadn't mentioned she was an heiress. Was she just as cognizant as he of men's less than altruistic motives when it came to dating her?

Who knew they had so much in common?

It certainly eased Vaughn's fears about revealing his true identity to her, when she was clearly rich several times over. It made what he was about to do very easy.

"I'm so excited you're in town," Sasha Charles told Miranda when they met for lunch at noon. Miranda was excited to finally spend time with her dear friend. Since college, they'd only seen each other on the odd girls' weekend, but to have quality time to seriously catch up was worth the trip to San Diego alone.

"Me too," Miranda responded. "It seems like I haven't seen you in ages."

Sasha laughed. "It has been a while. The last time I saw you was when we went to that ski chalet in Colorado with our significant others."

Miranda rolled her eyes. She remembered that trip and how she'd been besotted with Anthony, all the while he'd been looking at other women in skintight ski outfits. What a fool she'd been. And she was determined not to make the mistakes of the past. She'd narrowly avoided disaster with Vic, but luckily she'd led with her head instead of her libido. Otherwise, all she would have had to show for her efforts was a good lay. Now, she could continue her search for a husband.

"Miranda?"

"Hmm…" She glanced up from her reverie to see Sasha watching her suspiciously. Her large brown eyes drew Miranda in as they always did. Her best friend looked put together in a conservative pencil skirt and white buttondown top. Sasha was a head taller than Miranda at five foot seven, with a shapely figure and the cutest pixie-like haircut she'd ever seen. Miranda had never done more than trim a few inches from her shoulder-length hair.

"What's going on?" When Miranda began to protest, Sasha held up her hand. "And before you give me some song and dance, remember that I know you. You can't keep secrets from me."

Miranda inwardly cringed. She was keeping one now. She hadn't revealed to Sasha the terms of her grandfather's will. She hadn't told anyone. It was embarrassing to find herself in the situation to begin with, let alone having people feel sorry for her that she couldn't find a man. She didn't want pity, not even from her best friend.

"I'm just trying to figure out my next move concerning my career," Miranda offered, which was a half-truth. "You know I haven't been happy for a while now. And I was hoping some time away would give me clarity on what to do next."

"You know what to do," Sasha replied. "Open your own B and B. You've been talking about it for as long as I can remember."

"It's not that simple. I need capital."

"Can't your parents loan you the money? Or what about a bank loan? I hate to see you giving up on your dreams." Sasha was a much sought-after marketing consultant.

Miranda frowned. "I'm not giving up. Just deciding on the best course of action." And once she had her hands on her inheritance, she would go after her dreams, full stop. She just needed a husband to get there. "Anyway, I was hoping maybe we could hit the town, maybe go to a happy hour and mingle."

"Really?" Sasha's brow rose a fraction. "Are you looking for a little vacation loving?"

Miranda laughed aloud. She could have easily have had that and then some last night. Vic had been one delicious male specimen who would have put a hurting on Miranda if she'd allowed him, but she hadn't. "I wouldn't mind a little company of the male persuasion."

"Well, then, let me look around," Sasha said, taking a forkful of her salad. "I'll text you and we'll make a night of it. Sound good?"

"Sure." But Miranda's brain drifted to Vic and the sensual smile he'd given her when he'd walked her to her hotel door. The way Vic had taken her in his arms and leaned into Miranda had her thinking about his hard length. *Why was she even thinking about a man who'd lied to her?* She needed to be sweeping him under the rug. So why did her heart burst with joy when his name came across her phone display several seconds later?

Last night, he'd taken her phone and input his number to be sure she wouldn't lose it and had insisted she do the same. He'd even rung the phone to ensure she hadn't given him a fake number. And now he was calling her.

She stared at the phone.

"Are you going to answer that?" Sasha inquired, inclining her head to the phone Miranda held in her palm.

She should ignore it, but another part of her wanted to answer and give Vic a piece of her mind. Swiping her thumb across her iPhone, she answered. "Hello."

"Hello, Miranda." *Why did his voice have to sound like hot fudge poured over a sundae?*

"Vic? Oh wait, I don't believe that's your real name, is it?" The words came tumbling out of Miranda's lips before she could stop them. Sasha stared back at her in confusion. Rising to her feet, she stepped away from the table for some privacy.

At the silence on the other end, she continued. "Cat got your tongue?"

A sigh sounded on the other end. "So you found out?"

"Uh, yes, I did. In this day and age, did you really expect I wouldn't discover the truth?"

"Honestly, I wasn't thinking that far in advance," he responded. "Another body part had taken over my brain."

Miranda colored at his meaning. "What are you hiding, Vic?"

"My bank account," he replied. "Same as you."

"What's that supposed to mean?"

"Miranda Jensen, trust fund baby of the Chicago Jensens, a prominent family in the finance world. Or at least that's what it said online."

So he'd researched her too? "Did you know who I was when you met me in the café?"

"No, just the opposite," Vaughn responded. "I knew nothing about you except that I'd met a beautiful woman that intrigued me, but I meet gorgeous women all the time. When you weren't forthcoming with information about yourself, it made me cagey, so I decided to look into your background."

"Why?"

"Because…similar to you, I've amassed a certain wealth and find myself watchful for gold diggers. I apologize that I wasn't honest with you, Miranda. I admit I'm a bit jaded by my past experiences. In any event, it's no excuse. And for the record, my real name is Vaughn Ellicott."

An apology? She hadn't expected that. And she now knew his given name. Vaughn. She kind of liked the sound of it.

"Wait a minute. Did you say you're wealthy?" He certainly wouldn't need a share of her inheritance if he had wealth of his own.

He snorted. "Don't sound so shocked. Just because I look like a surfer dude doesn't mean I don't work."

"Ouch." She touched her chest as she felt the sting of his words. "Of course you do. I guess I just thought you might be one of those guys with a contract or endorsements or something to surf full-time."

"You thought I was that good?" Surprise was evident in his voice.

Sasha motioned Miranda back over to the table but she shook her head and said. "I watched you for an hour. You know you're that good."

"I'm glad you think so. But I didn't call you for praise."

"Oh no? Why did you call?"

"So we could start again," Vaughn replied quickly. "I'd like a clean slate with you, Miranda. So you can get to know the real me. I called to ask you for a second date."

Miranda's heart lurched in excitement. She had enjoyed spending time in Vic's—no, Vaughn's—company, but he hadn't been forthright with her. Why should she go down that rabbit hole again? It wouldn't be prudent. "I don't think it's a good idea to see each other again."

"So who is lying now?"

"Excuse me?"

"We had a good time. And you and I both know that the night might have ended differently if you hadn't got cold feet."

"I didn't get cold feet. I just don't sleep around with men I barely know which clearly I didn't since you couldn't be bothered to give me your real name."

"Duly noted." He ignored her dig. "Now about that dinner? My treat, someplace nice and I promise I'll even dress up and everything." Miranda remembered the distressed jeans and T-shirt he'd worn that hugged his tight bottom and bulging biceps. He'd looked darn good to her. Was she ready to see this new wealthy Vaughn Ellicott and see him all spruced up?

Yes, she was. Even though she knew it was fruitless effort, she could enjoy one last evening with him before she began her husband-seeking mission again because he certainly wouldn't need a share of her inheritance.

"I take your silence as acquiescence, so I'll pick you up at your hotel at seven p.m. sharp. And Miranda?"

"Yes?"

"Wear something sexy." Seconds later, the line went dead and Miranda stared down at it in disbelief. Her circumstances had changed in mere seconds from being alone to a date with a fine man she was extremely attracted to.

Miranda walked back to the table and Sasha was staring at her wide-eyed. "Well?" Her brow raised a fraction. "Are you going to tell me what that was all about?"

Mirada shrugged. She didn't understand it herself. She should be running in the opposite direction from a charmer like Vaughn who'd brushed aside his dishonesty under the rug and got her to accept his dinner invite.

"Don't you dare? Spill."

Ten minutes later, Sasha was glancing at her in bewilderment as if she'd suddenly sprouted horns. "What?"

"You're going to give this guy another chance after he lied to you about something as simple as his name?"

"Why not?" Miranda shrugged. It wasn't as if she had men lined up at her door. Plus she was about to tie herself down in marriage for the next year. Why not enjoy what could be the final night of her freedom? "He explained why he was less than honest when we met. He's encountered a lot of gold diggers, just like I have. If anyone can understand I can. Plus, he's attractive as hell."

"Yeah, I know," Sasha replied. "Vaughn Ellicott is considered quite the commodity in San Diego, but no woman has ever captured his heart. The man is a notorious playboy. About the only thing he can commit to is the ocean and his fascination with surfing."

"Who's to say I need him to commit?" *Though that's exactly what she needed.* "Perhaps I just want someone to spend some time with? It's not easy being alone."

"Of course not, sweetie. I just want someone worthy of you."

Miranda sighed heavily. She might have found one, a man who didn't care about how many zeros she had in her bank account because he had plenty to go around on his own. Which meant she was no closer to finding her husband than she'd been twenty-four hours ago.

Chapter 3

The evening came quick and Vaughn was happy it did. Once he'd discovered that he had no reason to fear that Miranda was after his money, he felt relieved. After they'd talked, Vaughn spent the remainder of the afternoon at the beach riding the waves like he'd stolen something. Then he'd returned to his home in La Jolla for a hot shower. Donning his favorite navy suit, Italian loafers and a splash of cologne, he was ready for the night.

Opening his five-car garage, Vaughn stared at the various vehicles. He wasn't in the mood for the Ferrari tonight. He certainly didn't need the Humvee. Or the Bugatti. No, tonight, he intended to woo and he knew just the vehicle. He reached inside the custom-made cabinet that housed all the keys to his babies and started toward his Rolls-Royce Phantom. Vaughn walked over, hopped in and, when the engine purred to life, he zipped out of the garage.

Was he trying to impress Miranda? Maybe just a little. Usually he was a take-it-or-leave-it kind of guy, but for some odd reason, he wanted Miranda's approval. Wanted her to see him with new eyes and as a viable catch she wouldn't mind having on her arm *or* in her bed.

He arrived promptly at 7:00 p.m. He pulled up to the hotel's entrance and found Miranda outside waiting for him. What had she thought was going to happen if he knocked on her door? Or maybe she didn't trust herself if they were alone in a room together? The anticipation of *what if* caused Vaughn to exit his Rolls-Royce with a bit more pep in his step than usual as he approached her.

He glanced at his Piaget watch. "Punctual. I like it."

Miranda shrugged. "It's a habit."

"One I like." He opened the passenger door for her to get in, but she turned to him.

"A Rolls?" She grinned as she slid in. "Nice touch."

Vaughn grinned like a Cheshire cat as he closed the door and strode to the driver's side. He glanced over at Miranda and took a moment to enjoy the expanse of leg on display thanks to the side slit. The woman had legs that went on for miles. Maybe one day those very legs would be wrapped around him as he brought them to sweet completion. Just then, Miranda glanced up and caught his appreciative gaze, but turned away.

Vaughn wasn't sure she was ready for him yet, but at least for tonight, she was his.

Miranda swallowed the frog in her throat as San Diego whirled by. She had no idea where Vaughn was taking her and she wasn't worried. She suspected it was going to be someplace chic because he'd told her to dress up. Or rather told her to wear something "sexy." She'd opted for an off-the-shoulder formfitting red dress with ruffled sleeves and a hem that hit above her knee. Miranda didn't want to give him any ideas that she was catering to his male fantasies. She'd worn the dress for her because it showed off her shoulders and figure, but left enough to the imagination.

Or had she?

Wasn't just a tiny part of her excited at the hungry gazes Vaughn bestowed upon her moments ago? He had been unable to hide his appreciation of her outfit. And Miranda had to admit that she'd gone the extra mile to ensure she looked spectacular tonight. She'd had her hair styled at the salon downstairs so that it now hung in soft curls down her back. The makeup artist had subtly accentuated her eyes, the curve of her lips and her high cheekbones. Overall, she was pleased with the result which made it appear as if she'd gone to little or no effort for the evening when it was quite the opposite.

With his eyes on the road, Miranda allowed herself a moment to hazard a glance at Vaughn's sinfully masculine face. Tonight, he looked much different than the casual Vic from last night. He looked more like an authority than the easygoing surfer with a zest for life. His suit was dark and tailored to fit like armor and accentuated every inch of his fit and trim six-foot physique. She was sure it had to have been custom made for him. He was every bit the assured businessman she'd researched online this afternoon, who'd come from a proud military family.

After lunch with Sasha ended, Miranda had pulled out her iPad and put Vaughn Ellicott into the search engine. She'd been shocked by the results. A former Navy man turned businessman. His surf gear business, Elite, had started out as a one-man operation, but having garnered contracts with several surfing associations to solely provide their gear, it had quickly morphed into a million-dollar company almost overnight. Vaughn Ellicott had a substantial fortune behind him.

Her practical side told Miranda to forget about Vaughn and focus on finding a man who could be bought, but her feminine side wasn't ready to let the sexy surfer go. And so, she'd agreed to a second date as a final hoorah. When it was over, she would return to her husband hunting search. For tonight, however, she would indulge her fantasy of what it would be like if she was free from restrictions and could have this man.

"We're here," Vaughn said, when he smoothly pulled up along the curb.

A valet opened Miranda's car door and she exited.

Vaughn came around and met her, sliding his arm around her waist as he led her inside the building. Miranda had to admit that she liked how he took charge. He led her to the elevator which took them to the twelfth floor.

"Reservation for Ellicott," Vaughn told the maître d' when they entered the restaurant housed there.

"Right this way, Mr. Ellicott." The portly man walked them through the elegantly appointed restaurant with views of San Diego and the bay at their feet.

"This place is amazing," Miranda commented once they were seated with a view of the San Diego skyline. She'd never heard of Mr. A's, but knew she'd be talking about it to Sasha later. Who would have anticipated such a jewel on the top floor of an office building?

"Only the best for you," Vaughn replied smoothly.

"Great line."

The waitress came over and Vaughn selected an expensive bottle of red wine from their black label wine list. Miranda knew it cost a mint because it was one of her father's favorites.

When she departed, Vaughn was wearing a frown. "I didn't give you a line earlier. I wanted to take you to someplace special after last night's chill atmosphere. Show you there's more to me than just what I portray outwardly."

"So you were acting last night?" She'd thought he'd been real with her, but if he wasn't she could hightail it out the door now. She'd been there and done that.

"Not at all, but if I'm honest—" He paused. "I had my guard up. Sometimes I don't know the type of woman I'm meeting and whether they want to spend time with me for me or because I'm a millionaire mogul."

Miranda released a sigh of relief. Maybe her radar wasn't completely as off as she thought. She'd read that he was part of an organization called Prescott George, but had been dubbed by the media as the Millionaire Moguls. "Tell me about Prescott George."

"How much did you read up on me this afternoon?" His sharp eyes bore into hers from across the table.

Miranda shrugged. "Enough, so don't skirt around the issue. I'd like to know more."

"I've been part of the organization for five years. My father, Vaughn Ellicott, Sr., has been a member for decades, but it was only when I left the Navy and started my own business and began giving back to the community that I got an invitation to join."

"So not anyone can join?"

"We're selective. Keeps the riffraff out."

Miranda chuckled.

"Prescott George is all about giving back to those less fortunate and lending a helping hand to the African-American community."

"I'm impressed," Miranda said. And she didn't say that often. They may have started out rocky with Vaughn not being honest with her, but he did seem to have integrity and she respected him and the work Prescott George did. If she was fortunate enough to get her hands on her inheritance, it wouldn't all go to starting her bed-and-breakfast. She too would give back.

"And you, Miranda?" Vaughn said. "Tell me more about what makes you tick. I suspect that I barely scratched the surface last night."

"I'm really quite easy. I went to school back east at Brown University. Received my MBA. However, rather than working at Jensen Finance I chose to work in the hotel business. Since graduating, I've been working my way up the ladder. Not at the pace I'd like, but I'll get there."

"Hmmm…that's all info I can probably find out online," he responded. "I want to know about you. Why are you still single? And more importantly, why are you in

San Diego when all your family and fortune is in Chicago? What gives? I feel like there's more to the story than you're telling me."

Miranda didn't like being put on the hot seat and a torrent of emotions surged up inside her. She didn't particularly want to discuss her personal life. Or the bad choices she'd made in the past. If she did, she might dig herself into a ditch and reveal too much about her plan and the real reason she was in San Diego. So she opted for a version of the truth. "I'm single because I have a penchant for picking the wrong man," she finally answered.

"Ah, you've intrigued me. Why do you think that is?"

"I don't know. Maybe they choose me too. They see a wealthy heiress and easy target."

"Don't sell yourself short," Vaughn replied. "Because that's not what I see."

"What do you see?"

He leaned forward and his long-lashed dark eyes stared into hers. It was impossible not to be completely mesmerized by his smoldering good looks. "I see a beautiful, vivacious and sexy woman that I want to spend time with and who I think finds me equally attractive."

Or at least he hoped so. Vaughn was surprised by how much he enjoyed Miranda's company. He thought about the beautiful model he'd dated a couple of months ago. And before her, he'd been with a dancer, yet none of those women held his attention for more than a few weeks at a time. Miranda on the other hand wasn't looking at how many zeros were in his bank account because she had plenty of her own. And for once, Vaughn could be at ease and let his guard down. "You do find me attractive, don't you?"

"Fishing for compliments?" Miranda inquired, sipping on her wine. "I would think a man as active as you wouldn't need them."

"Excuse me?"

"I'm not blind," she responded. "I saw the articles about your dating conquests. You have quite the active social life and the reputation to go along with it."

The waitress returned and took their dinner orders so Vaughn didn't comment until after she'd left. "I do, but none of them have intrigued me as much as you do."

"Do you always speak so frankly?"

He smiled. "Yes, I do. And I want to know more about you. What about your family?"

"My parents, Tucker and Leigh, live in Chicago. My father is the CEO of the Jensen Financial Group and my mother is content to stay at home and be a socialite." Her voice raised a fraction. "We're pretty boring and nothing much to tell."

"I doubt that. Brothers or sisters?"

She shook her head. "Nope. Just me. I'm an only child."

A grin spread across his sinful lips. "Were you spoiled rotten?"

"Surprisingly, no, my parents never deigned to give me my heart's desire. Instead, they taught me about hard work and dedication to achieve one's goals."

"Sounds like my family," Vaughn concurred. "My father, the Commander, didn't believe in handing anything to us. We had to work for it. And in my case join the Navy as he did and his father before him."

"And your sisters? What do they do?"

"My sisters Emily and Brianne are both married with children and live here in San Diego. Until recently, my baby sister, Eliza, owned a fashion boutique in New York, but she's since opened a boutique here in her hometown. I'm very proud of her."

"You're close to your family?"

"Yes, I am. I find they keep me grounded and never let all the wealth and prestige get to my head."

They continued leisurely talking over a three-course meal of Maine lobster strudel with Cognac lobster sauce; duck confit with huckleberry sauce and orange reduction followed by a decadent dessert of salted caramel and chocolate bar with a peanut praline crisp which they shared. Vaughn was enjoying the night so much he didn't want it to end. He suggested coffee on the outdoor terrace and that was where they stayed until late when he drove Miranda to her hotel.

Vaughn was reluctant for the evening to end. Miranda was a gorgeous woman and throughout the evening his gaze would fix on her silky brown skin that he'd love to touch, or drift to her lush pink-tinted lips. She'd dressed for him tonight, of that he was sure. The dress with its ruffled sleeves accentuated her shapely figure without showing too much. It stopped at her knee, revealing a tantalizing amount of leg, and the neckline gave a tempting view of her full cleavage.

He was desperate to take her upstairs to her room, yet was afraid of coming on too strong, but damn if he couldn't picture the two of them making passionate sweet love all night long. Miranda wanted it too. She hadn't shied away when his hand had covered hers on the restaurant terrace. In fact, he'd felt her breath hitch at his touch. Or complained when he'd come behind her and slid his arms on either side of her as he'd pointed out several points of interest. In fact, he could have sworn she'd sniffed him, inhaling his scent much as he'd done hers. Miranda's sweet yet subtle perfume had oozed over his senses, filling his nostrils and seducing his mind into wanting to do all kinds of things to her body.

Miranda was taking him to new dimensions, but she was reluctant to speed up their relationship to the next level. Vaughn was accustomed to women who were a lot more confident and went after what they wanted. Women who gave him hungry stares so he knew what was offered. But Miranda seemed innocent, fragile even. He would have to handle her with care.

When the Rolls-Royce came to a stop in front of the hotel, Vaughn flew out the car, eager to open Miranda's door since the valet was preoccupied with another customer. He lent her his hand and she slid out from the vehicle.

"Thank you."

The valet came toward him. "What room?" he inquired, peering at Vaughn.

Vaughn was silent. He would take his cue from Miranda. If she gave him her room number, it meant he'd be staying the night and finally capitalizing on the lust that had been coursing through him since he'd laid eyes on her at the beach.

She glanced up, her eyes scanning his dark ones. He wanted her, but it had to be her choice. "Room eleven zero eight."

The valet nodded and Vaughn watched as he hopped inside the vehicle and pulled away from the curb. Grasping Miranda's hand, they walked through the lobby to the elevator bank. Once inside, awareness exploded between them and Vaughn nearly stopped breathing. Miranda was standing opposite him and he was mesmerized by the shape of her face and her delicately carved lips. So much so that it didn't escape his attention when her tongue nervously darted out to moisten her lips. His whole body tightened in male response because he wanted to take her tongue in his mouth and suck on it voraciously. And he would, once he was inside her room.

When her eyes fastened on his, he noticed her pupils were dilated as if she too were acknowledging the palpable tension in the air. If he wasn't mistaken, he saw her tremble just as the door chime indicated they'd reached her floor. They walked hand-in-hand to her hotel room and once they reached her door, Miranda pulled out her card and handed it to him.

He accepted it and used it to open the door. Miranda walked inside and he followed, for the first time unsure if this was the right thing. As much as his libido was raging, Vaughn wanted Miranda to be comfortable taking their relationship further. But instead of pulling away, she surprised him when she walked forward and pushed him backward, shutting the door. Her arms curved around his neck and he could see a tiny pulse beating in her throat as his entire body came alive at having her delicious body against his.

Then all Vaughn could feel was fire as Miranda bent her head and touched her lips to his. Her mouth was warm and sweet and his senses exploded, making him take control of the kiss. He claimed her lips, filling himself with her as he'd wanted to do the last two days, but had been unable to. Blood pounded in his veins as pure unadulterated lust slithered through him. Vaughn couldn't recall a time when the passion he'd felt for a woman had been this raging hot, threatening to scorch him.

From a distance, he heard her whimper of desire and then her fingers curled around his neck.

Miranda forgot everything and anything in the moment but Vaughn. She didn't know what had possessed her to give the valet her room number, but in that single action she'd made it clear to Vaughn that he was welcome to stay for the evening. Even more unusual was her handing him her hotel room card and kissing him first.

But she was glad she had.

Otherwise she would never know what it was like to be properly kissed. Vaughn's arm curved around her waist, drawing her closer to him and his arousal. It sent shivers of delight through Miranda that she could turn a man like Vaughn on. Her last two relationships had shaken her confidence in her ability to keep the opposite sex interested. Having Anthony cheat on her and Chris only date for her money had left her feeling vulnerable, but the heated caress of Vaughn's gaze all evening had obliterated any doubt of how he felt.

She fell deep into the kiss. Enjoyed the erotic slide of his tongue in and out of her mouth. His kiss was hot and hungry as his tongue slid more firmly inside her to explore every inch of her mouth with skilled mastery. When he pulled away to nip her ear with his teeth or glide his deliciously wet tongue against her throat or suck her neck with ravaging pulls, wondrous feelings erupted inside. Her breasts began to ache for his touch especially when he pressed her lower back toward him. She could feel the hard ridge of his erection pushing against her pelvis and it caused molten heat to pool between her thighs.

No words were uttered between them. Instead his fingers combed through her hair, from root to tip, and his hands splayed across her backside, hips and thighs. She gasped when he ground the steel of his manhood against her melting core and began rubbing against her. He was imprinting himself on every inch of her body. And Miranda was powerless to his onslaught. Instead she rode the wave, her breasts swelling in response and her nipples turning into pebbles underneath the sheer fabric of the chiffon dress. He had to know how horny he was making her, but he wasn't pushing her backward on the bed. Instead, he rolled her nipples between his fingers until they turned to buds and then he pushed the fabric of her dress down so he could close his lips around one nipple through her strapless bra. He suckled her so strongly that a moan of pleasure escaped her lips as he lashed the turgid point with hot strokes of his tongue.

Miranda writhed in his hold and whimpered when his mouth left her breast to return and plunder her mouth. His tongue invaded hers and she dueled with him for supremacy. It was like she was having an out-of-body experience and she was no longer herself. Who was this wanton creature taking what Vaughn was so boldly giving her? He was sliding her down his body with leisurely movements, forcing her to ride his erection through their clothing. Moans escaped her lips followed by sharp intakes of breath. The center of her was throbbing and only Vaughn could assuage it.

This was no slow seduction because no doubt about it, Vaughn had been seducing her all night. First with the compliments, the fancy dinner, watching the moonlight on the terrace. It had all been to seduce her senses and he'd succeeded. She was a frenzy of need. She wanted him… to do anything and everything to her. But if she allowed that to happen, if she made love with this man, no matter how satisfying it would be—tomorrow she would still be in the exact same place without a husband. And Vaughn would walk away with a smug smile in the morning, leaving her alone just as every other man before him had done.

Miranda began pushing her hands against his chest, letting him know that they had to end this. It took several seconds, but slowly Vaughn eased his hold and lowered her back to the ground.

Dear heaven, what had she done?

Embarrassed at just how far she'd allowed things to go between them, Miranda quickly lifted her dress, backed up, spun away from him and walked toward the window.

"Miranda, are you alright?" Vaughn inquired from behind her. His voice was husky with desire.

She nodded. This was her fault. She'd made a mistake when she'd allowed him to come back to her room. Once again, she was falling for the wrong man. In an alternate universe in which she wasn't looking down the barrel of a gun to get inheritance, Vaughn could have been the right man, but he wasn't. There was no incentive for a man as rich as Vaughn to marry her. She had to find someone else desperate and willing to marry her for a year, but who?

Because as much as she might like to have finished what they started, Vaughn was never going to be that man.

Vaughn stared at Miranda's rigid back as she faced the window. His body hummed with unfulfilled tension, his manhood ached and throbbed with a need to mate with this woman. He took a deep breath, struggling for control. *What the hell was happening to him?* He'd always considered himself a disciplined man who allowed himself the odd indulgence, but Miranda was so provocatively tempting, she was forcing him to basic near primitive instincts.

It was clear that the evening was over. He just had to extricate himself with as much diplomacy and tact as possible while still allowing Miranda to save face. He knew she had to feel horrible enough without his anger as a factor. And he was angry because she was fighting their attraction. But yet he could see she was conflicted. Her mind was telling her to walk away, but her body—her body wanted him something fierce. The way she'd ridden his shaft had him in desperate need of a cold shower. *Pronto.*

But she also seemed to warring with herself about what was right and wrong. He would do the right thing. "I should go."

Slowly, she pivoted on her heel to face him. The strained look on her face told him she was thankful. "I think that might best. I should never have allowed you to come up. Should never have gotten involved."

"How can you say that, Miranda? When you and I so clearly complement each other."

She took a step backward and he could sense her pulling further away from him. "I'm sorry for giving you mixed signals and for giving you the wrong idea that I—I wanted…" She didn't say another word; instead she rushed off to the bathroom and slammed the door, effectively shutting him out.

He walked to the door and placed his ear against it, but all he could hear was sniffles. "Miranda. Miranda?" When she continued to remain silent, Vaughn released a long sigh. "Okay, I'll go, but I just want you to know that the time we've spent together the last couple of evenings has been nothing short of spectacular and I hope to see you again."

He placed his hand on the door. And after willing it to open for several more seconds, he finally gave up, opened the hotel room door and left.

Chapter 4

Vaughn glanced at the clock on the nightstand and watched the minutes tick by past 2:00 a.m. He was anxious, impatient, angry and downright mystified by Miranda's reaction. He thought about how her huge brown eyes had looked tonight when she'd walked toward him, her arms encircling his neck as she'd laid one helluva kiss on him. It didn't make any sense. One minute she was hot with desire for him and the next minute she was cold as ice, sending him away from her hotel room for the *second* night in a row. How was it possible that this beautiful stranger he'd only just met had him tied up in knots? Even more so, because now he knew what she tasted like. He remembered the way she'd kissed him back when he'd explored every nook and crevice of her deliciously sinful mouth. A mouth that was made for loving. His loving.

But she'd rejected him. Denying them both the satisfaction they both craved.

Why? The little sounds and moans she'd made as she'd ridden his shaft had told Vaughn exactly how much she wanted him. He should probably walk away and move on to another woman. An easier choice, who was confident enough in herself to take what she wanted, regardless of the consequences. But Miranda wasn't that woman. Something was holding her back and he had to know why she was running scared; only then could he make peace with the situation. And, if necessary, allow himself to move on.

As if that were possible.

He'd never wanted another woman as achingly as he wanted Miranda and it wasn't just because she'd turned him down either. He loved her independent streak and how she spoke of starting her own business, but there was also an innocence and vulnerability he saw in her that appealed to every male instinct in him to protect. Protect her.

Vaughn waited until a reasonable hour of the morning and after showering, he grabbed a mug of coffee from his favorite coffee house and headed for Miranda's hotel. He was determined to get answers.

When he arrived, he tossed his keys at the valet and went straight for the elevators. He was halfway there when a mane of luscious black hair caught his attention. Vaughn stopped dead in his tracks. Miranda was at the front desk with a suitcase! He marched toward her.

"Hello, Miranda."

Startled, she spun around on her heel. "V-Vaughn? W-what are you doing here?"

Miranda was stunned to see Vaughn standing behind her. When she'd looked up, her stomach dissolved into a familiar flutter at the sight of him. He was casually dressed in jeans and a T-shirt showing off his honed muscular body. She felt her throat go parched as she stared at the sensual curve of his mouth. A mouth that had darn near given her an orgasm last night. The way his lips had sucked her neck as his fingers had drifted over her bare legs had made her feel incredibly wanton.

"Ms. Jensen, here's your bill." The hotel clerk interrupted her lascivious thoughts and slid the bill across the counter.

Miranda turned around. "Thank you." She glanced down at the charges, but hardly saw them because she could feel Vaughn's rising anger from behind her and her skin prickled with guilt. He knew she'd been leaving without telling him goodbye. "The bill appears in order."

"Very well, then. We'll charge it to the card on file?"

Miranda nodded. She glanced behind her to see if Vaughn was still there, and he was. His hands were folded across his impressive chest and she could see he was not moving a muscle without an explanation. Once she'd concluded her transaction, Miranda reached for her suitcase, but Vaughn beat her to the punch and wheeled it away to a sofa in a secluded area of the lobby, where they could no doubt talk in private.

He motioned for her to sit and she did, while Vaughn opted for the chair beside her. She didn't like it because she was caged in by Vaughn's legs and the cocktail table. "So, Miranda, do you want to tell me why you were high-tailing it out of town?"

"I've completed my business here," she said. "It's time for me to move on."

His brow furrowed. "Is that a fact?"

"It is." She straightened her shoulders. But even as she said the words, they both knew it was a lie.

She was leaving because Vaughn had gotten too close. When he was around, Miranda couldn't think clearly. She only felt. Felt things she shouldn't. Couldn't afford to feel. She'd been preoccupied with this man for the last forty-eight hours. She'd been listless and distracted thinking about how he'd taken her in his arms and the excitement he made her feel. Last night, she'd been unable to sleep, remembering the passionate kissing and touching they'd shared in her room. She hadn't been able to push the thoughts away and she was angry with herself for losing focus on her goal of finding a husband.

"That's bull and you know it, Miranda," Vaughn responded. "You're leaving because you're running scared. And I haven't the faintest idea why."

"That's because you have no idea what I'm dealing with." Miranda rose to her feet and so did Vaughn. "I have to go. I have a plane to catch." She tried unsuccessfully to push past him, but all she was greeted with was a rock-hard wall of chest. "Move aside, Vaughn."

"Not until you tell me what's going on," he said. "And I think now is as good a time as any." He grabbed her suitcase and took her other hand with his free hand and led her toward the exit.

"What do you think you're doing," she asked, nearly trotting to keep up with his long strides. "You can't just manhandle me."

"I can. And I will," he said tightly. He handed the valet his ticket and she watched him scurry to get Vaughn's vehicle.

Vaughn's grip on her loosened, but instead of letting her go, he laced his fingers through hers. Miranda stared down at their joined hands. It was an innocent action, but held so much meaning. "I'm not letting you go," he whispered, looking down at her. "Otherwise, I fear you'll run in the opposite direction. So you'll stay with me until you tell me the real reason you're running and keeping me at arm's length."

They stood in relative silence, each in their own thoughts until the valet returned with Vaughn's car several minutes later. Once Vaughn had ushered her inside the passenger side and put her luggage in his trunk, he got in the driver's seat. "Buckle up, Miranda. Something tells me we're in for a ride."

Vaughn was positively livid. He'd seen red when he'd found Miranda at the front desk about to sneak out on him. His groin had also hardened when he saw her in those skinny jeans and a peasant top. The denim hugged every curve of her tight, round bottom and he was eager to run his hands along her backside, but resisted the urge. The look she'd given him when he'd caught her red-handed was nothing short of deer in the headlights and he didn't want that. He wanted her relaxed and pliable.

Like she'd been last night when she'd nearly come apart in his arms.

"Where are you taking me?" she inquired.

"To my office. We'll have relative quiet there since it's the weekend."

"Why couldn't you have just let me go? There's so much more going on here than you know."

"And I'm eager to hear all about it."

"What if I don't want to tell you?" She pressed her lips together in anger.

He took his eyes off traffic long enough to reply. "You will." Then he returned his focus to the road.

"You're awfully arrogant. Why would I confide in you?"

"I think you're desperate to tell someone and get whatever it is off your chest."

She was silent. Had he accurately assessed her? Vaughn would soon find out. Her hotel wasn't far from Elite's headquarters and he was pulling into his reserved parking space fifteen minutes later.

Miranda jumped out of the car without waiting for him to open her door and glanced around at her surroundings.

"What?"

She shrugged. "I guess I just assumed your offices would be at the beach."

He grinned as he walked toward the double doors. "I do run a business." He unlocked the door and held it open for her. "But we're not far."

She glanced up at him, her mouth curving into an unconscious smile. "I wouldn't think so." Then she strutted inside.

Vaughn couldn't resist watching her fanny as he followed her into the converted loft space and turned the lights on. "Would you like some coffee?"

"Would love some."

While he set about making coffee in the state-of-the-art kitchen which housed a large countertop that often held their catered health-conscious lunches, Vaughn watched Miranda walk around his two-story office. She seemed to marvel at the rafters and open concept. When he was finished with the coffee, he brought over two mugs to Miranda, who'd made herself comfortable in an oversize chair overlooking the La Jolla Shores beach.

He sat beside her in the other and turned to her. "The floor is yours."

She took a sip of her coffee and said, "You're the one who kidnapped me. I never said I was going to tell you my life story."

He chuckled and reclined in his chair. "I think *kidnap* is a strong word, but I'm a friend with an ear to listen if you care to share."

Her brow shot in surprise. "Friend?" She mulled the word over on her lips as if it was foreign to her and then sipped her coffee in silence. Vaughn wondered if she was intent on keeping mum about whatever it was that was bothering her when she finally spoke. "I'm sorry for being a tease last night. It's just that I shouldn't have let you come up. No." She shook her head. "I shouldn't even have gone out with you to begin with. I have a lot on my plate right now."

"Such as?"

She sighed heavily and looked at him closely as if weighing her options. Could she trust him? Could she not? She must have chosen the latter because she put down her coffee mug and blurted out, "If I don't marry in the next month, I'm going to lose my inheritance."

"Excuse me?" Vaughn said. Now it was his turn to plop down his mug on the table, causing brown liquid to spill over.

"I should get a towel."

She rose to move, but he grabbed her arm. "Leave it! I want to know what you mean by that statement."

Her eyes glittered at him and there was no trace of humor in those brown depths. "You heard me correctly, Vaughn. Since my grandfather's death, I'm set to inherit millions as you've read online, but what no one knows is there's a condition to that inheritance."

"Which is?"

"That I must marry before my thirtieth birthday or forfeit my entire fortune to one of my grandfather's charities."

"Why on earth would he make *marriage* a condition of his will?"

"Because he was a spiteful old man, stuck in the Stone Age. He believed that a woman needs a man. And I obviously have made poor choices with men because of my three last disastrous relationships, one of which almost had me married to a gold digger. My grandfather felt like I needed looking after and this is his way of ensuring that happens."

"But that's positively medieval!"

"Don't you think I know that?" Miranda's voice rose several octaves and she stood up and began pacing the tile floor. "But there's no way around it. Trust me, I've been looking for a way out over the last two months since his death and neither I or my lawyers can find one."

"So what are you going to do?"

"I took a leave of absence from my job in Chicago and decided to go hunting for a husband."

"And you came here to San Diego? I would think there would be a lot more choices in Chicago. You're a beautiful woman, Miranda. I find it hard to believe that men aren't lining up at your door."

Miranda rolled her eyes upward. "Well, they weren't. I wasn't having much luck in Chicago, so I came to San Diego. My best friend, Sasha, lives here and I thought it might help to have a friendly face around."

Vaugh rose to his feet, shaking his head. "Wow, this all seems so unreal. That your grandfather would do this to you. When is your thirtieth birthday?"

She glanced down at her watch. "Two days ago, I had a month left. And now, I have exactly twenty-eight days."

"Sweet Jesus!"

"My plan was to find a man and make him an offer he couldn't refuse, a hefty paycheck if he stays married to me for one year."

"And after the one year?"

"We go our separate ways."

Vaughn rubbed his goatee as he mulled over her words. Miranda was willing to marry a complete stranger to get access to her fortune? How did she know they could be trusted? She could get herself in a world of trouble if she made this offer to just *any* man. He feared the scoundrels she'd find who were out to make a fast buck. She could be hurt, physically as well as emotionally. What the hell was she thinking? Her plan was outrageous!

"Can't you see now why I've been so conflicted?" Miranda asked, looking at him. "Yes, I find myself attracted to you, but I also have to look at my future. And that inheritance is a way for me to preserve my independence, to have the bed-and-breakfast I told you about. I can't just let those dreams and goals go because I'm hot for a surfer."

Vaughn spun around and surveyed her brown eyes. Miranda hadn't meant for that comment to slip. She drained the contents of her coffee mug and brought it over to the kitchen sink to rinse it out. She seemed nervous and edgy as she stood by the counter putting distance between them.

"So you admit you wanted to make love with me?" His voice was a low drawl as he walked over to her in the kitchen. He had her exactly where he wanted her. She was finally confessing that she wanted him and he could capitalize on it.

"Th-that's not what I said," she stammered when he reached her and placed an arm on either side of the counter, boxing her in. "I said I was attracted to you."

Vaughn grinned. How could she honestly stand there and let the lie escape her lips when it was evident in her eyes right now that she wanted him? Her eyes begged him to kiss her. "Do you care to prove if that were true?" He hauled her to him until her lips were inches away from his.

"Vaughn, don't," she protested, squirming in his arms.

He grazed his lips lightly over hers, giving her just a taste of what she'd sampled last night.

"Please don't…"

"Don't what?"

"Seduce me," she said. "Because you know that's what you want to do, could do, and with a little coercion maybe I would cave and you'd have me in your bed, but it would still put me right back where I am. I need a husband and I'm quickly running out of time to find one."

His grip loosened and she slid out of his embrace. She walked away from him and back to the chairs facing the ocean. She was between a rock and a hard place. There was no way she was going to find a man good enough to marry her in this short amount of time. At least not an honorable man who would do the right thing by her, and she deserved that. He may not have known her long, but Miranda was a special lady. Soft, gentle and kind, and the wrong man would and could certainly take advantage of her naïveté.

She needed someone to protect her.

She needed *him*.

"You're awfully quiet," she responded. "I thought you had a quick comeback for everything?"

Vaughn stared at her for several long moments. He knew what he had to do. And he was the best man for the job. He walked toward her and when he reached her chair, he dropped down to one knee and said, "Marry me."

Chapter 5

"What did you say?" Surely, Miranda hadn't heard him correctly. Because if she had, it would be the answer to her prayers.

"You heard me. Marry me."

Her eyes grew wide with amazement. "Just like that? You're offering to marry me, but that's crazy. Why would you do such a thing? You certainly don't need the money. You have loads of it. And let's not forget about your reputation with the ladies. I'm sure there's plenty of females wanting to be Mrs. Ellicott."

"But I didn't propose to any of those females," he responded. "I proposed to you, Miranda Jensen. Now are you going to say yes, so I can get off my knee?"

Miranda grasped Vaughn by the arm, helping him from the floor. She glanced up at him as she contemplated his offer, trying to figure out his motives, but there didn't appear to be any. Instead, there was a hopeful glint in his eyes. "You don't have to do this, Vaughn."

"I know that. I *want* to do it."

"You want to get married?" She didn't believe it for a second. He was a notorious bachelor.

"Listen, we can both benefit from this arrangement."

"How so?"

"For starters, it would help me with my business if I had a wife as fine as you on my arm." Miranda couldn't resist feeling warm inside at the compliment. "Plus, it would relieve some pressure I've been getting from my family over my bachelor status. My mother is eager to see me married in the hopes that some grandchildren will follow."

"Grandchildren?" Miranda croaked. "You do realize that this would be a short-term arrangement?"

"Of course, I do, but it'll get them off my back for a while. So you see? It's a win-win for both of us. You get your inheritance and my family will feel better thinking I've settled down."

"Speaking of inheritance…" Miranda hated to bring it up, but she had to know what exactly his terms were. "What do you want for agreeing to this marriage?"

Vaughn grinned wickedly.

Miranda could see the lascivious thoughts running through his mind. And she was torn. She'd never been so powerfully attracted to a man before, which could make this arrangement a very bad idea if sex was put in the mix. On the other hand, a man was standing in front of her, offering her a way out of this entire fiasco. "I meant in terms of a financial incentive. I've willing to compensate you quite generously for giving up a year of your life."

This time, a frown replaced the sexy smirk on his face. "I'm insulted you would even think I'd take it, Miranda. As you've said, I don't need the money. I'm quite wealthy in my own right and I won't take what's rightfully yours."

"Then what?" Her voice rose. "What do you possibly get out of this?"

You, Vaughn thought as he stared back at Miranda, but he couldn't possibly say that to her. Not right now. She was already on the fence about his offer of marriage. As soon as she'd told him of her predicament, he'd known he couldn't let Miranda venture off to find some random stranger to be her husband, not when he was more than suitable for the position. Sure, he hadn't exactly been looking for a wife, but he knew in the future at some point, he'd get married and have a wife and a couple of children. He was just accelerating his time line.

Miranda needed him, but that was only one of his reasons for marrying her. If he told her he wanted her in his bed, on top of his bed or anywhere else of his choosing, she'd run as fast as she could *away* from him. He wanted her to come to him willingly.

"Well?" she asked. "Because all I can offer you is a marriage of convenience."

Vaughn chuckled inwardly. She was letting him know in no uncertain terms that sex was no part of that equation. Clearly, Miranda was having short-term memory loss because Vaughn hadn't been able to forget the heat that had nearly scorched them last night and they'd only got to first base. "We'll see."

"Excuse me?"

"I'm attracted to you, Miranda, and you've already admitted the feeling is mutual, but if it'll help you come to grips with our arrangement, then yes, our marriage will be platonic. I've never had to force myself on a woman before and I'm not about to start now. So we'll only make love when you come to me." There. He'd thrown down the gauntlet and put the ball in her court. Now it was up to Miranda to decide if she could live with their terms.

Miranda stared at him in disbelief, but she held out her hand. "It's a deal. I'll marry you."

Vaughn grasped her hand in his. He was getting a beautiful, sexy wife and it was just a matter of time before she would come to his bed.

Their first order of business that afternoon was getting Miranda checked back into her hotel while their respective lawyers drew up the papers detailing their arrangement. Vaughn hadn't cared that it was the weekend; his lawyers were on retainer and he expected them to be available twenty-four seven if a critical situation arose. Miranda needed to stay married to Vaughn for one year in order to keep her fortune. Vaughn agreed to the stipulation because it met with his goals, but he had no intention of going that long being celibate. He understood Miranda's need to feel like she was in control of her own destiny even though her grandfather was pulling the strings. Vaughn had felt similar once upon a time. When he'd been in the Navy, he'd been at the will of the United States government and his father, but not anymore.

He wasn't, however, giving in when it came to a wedding. Miranda was trying to convince him they should get married in secret.

"Let's just go to Vegas or to a justice of the peace," she suggested later when he came around to pick her up for dinner.

He and Miranda had opted for casual café fare. She'd changed into shorts and a flowing white top with the shoulders cut out. He hadn't been able to resist touching the delicate skin when he'd greeted with her a hug. He wished it would have been followed by a kiss, but Miranda was staying true to her look but don't touch rule. So tonight, all he could do was look his fill, but that didn't mean he was going to let her have her way. "We are not going to a justice of the peace, Miranda. We are having a real wedding."

"Why not?" Miranda's lips formed in a pout. "Why go through all the fuss of a wedding when our arrangement is far from real. Why have the added expense? My inheritance won't be available until after we wed, so I won't be able to help with the cost."

"Did I ask you to pay for it?"

Her brow furrowed. "Well, no, but I just assumed…"

"Well, you assumed wrong. I have everything under control. We will have a proper wedding as befitting a man of my standing and a member of Prescott George."

"Oh. I hadn't thought about that."

"No worries, but I do have a reputation to uphold. And part of the reason why our marriage benefits me is to take the pressure off me marrying. Once the community realizes I'm no longer available, the piranhas will look for other prey."

"Is that really how you see women?" she asked incredulously.

"Not all of them." His eyes pierced hers. He knew Miranda was nothing like those women who were looking to score a wealthy man to ensure they lived a lavish lifestyle. Or who were seeking to trip him up by getting pregnant. Once he'd actually caught one of his dates poking holes in the condoms before she'd put them back in the drawer on his nightstand. Maybe it was because Miranda had been born into wealth. Or maybe not. She didn't strike him as one of those greedy females. "Anyway, our marriage will work. You get what you want and I get what I want."

Not entirely though. He was going to have to be patient before he really got his heart's desire. Miranda Jensen in his arms.

"Alright, then you've convinced me. We'll have a big splashy wedding, but I'm going to need a dress."

He grinned. "I've got you covered there. My assistant, Kindra, has arranged an appointment for you at one of the most exclusive bridal boutiques in San Diego."

"Is that right? You seem to have it all figured out, but there's one thing you left out."

"And what's that?"

"Have you told your parents about our upcoming nuptials?"

Vaughn frowned. He hadn't and she knew that. "No, I haven't."

"Don't take too much time," she warned, "because I have a feeling they may not have the reaction you're envisioning."

* * *

Miranda was right. Vaughn didn't look forward to telling his parents about his sudden marriage. He and Miranda had each agreed to tell their parents separately and as he drove up the coast to the Ellicott family estate the next morning, Vaughn knew it wasn't going to be a pleasant conversation.

He was right.

Vaughn Ellicott, Sr. greeted him at the door with a handshake. His father, although not as tall as Vaughn, was a formidable-looking man at six feet with steely eyes as fathomless as the dark of night. His features were rugged and although not conventionally handsome, his father's confidence must have convinced Vaughn's mother, Natalie Ellicott, a quiet, unassuming woman, to fall for him. He had a deep, strong voice which he was making known after Vaughn followed him into the living room and greeted his mother with a kiss on the cheek and proceeded to fill them in on the reason for his visit.

"What is this about?" his father bellowed as his mouth curved into a frown. "Marriage to a stranger whom your mother and I—" he turned to his wife of four decades "—have never even met! Why, the idea is utterly ridiculous!"

Vaughn sucked in a deep breath and prepared for the onslaught. He'd known telling his parents wasn't going to be easy. That was why he'd opted to do it alone. He hadn't wanted to subject Miranda to his father's temper. And he'd been right.

"What? No smart comeback?" his father quipped.

"I know this is a shock…"

"Shock?" His father leaned forward on the sofa. "Shock is when something happens suddenly and without warning. This is deliberate. You're deliberately setting out to ruin your future."

Vaughn grimaced. Trust his father to throw the first blow. "That's not what I'm doing."

"Then what are you doing, sweetie?" His mother spoke. The softness of her tone caused him to stand down because Vaughn had been ready to tell his father a thing too.

At sixty-three, his mother was a beautiful woman with skin the color of nutmeg. Her oval face was delicately carved and her large expressive eyes always had a way of pulling Vaughn in. She was a meek woman no thanks to years of his father's dominant personality. Yet she carried herself regally and was always the height of sophistication wearing tailored slacks and a twin set with pearls.

"Miranda and I are eager to start our lives. I would think you both would be happy. For years, you've been pressuring me to settle down. Get a wife. Have a couple of kids." He repeated comments they'd made previously.

"We would be ecstatic if you weren't springing this on us all of a sudden and we'd gotten to know your fiancée. Why now? What's the rush?" she asked.

"Your mother's right. Did you knock the girl up? Is that why you're rushing to the altar without giving the family a chance to get to know her? Didn't I teach you how important it was to protect yourself against gold diggers? She's probably marrying you to get her hands on your money. You've amassed quite a bit of wealth."

"I'm surprised you'd noticed," Vaughn returned. "Considering you wanted me to stay in the Navy." And be like him. Well, no, thank you. Vaughn never wanted that kind of life.

His father glared at him. "Of course I noticed. And so has every other woman in the San Diego area."

"Your father's right, Vaughn. You're an eligible bachelor. The papers are always saying so. How do you know she's not after your money?"

"Because she has money of her own. A sizable inheritance."

"Then why not wait?" his mother implored. "Let us get to know her and vice versa. You haven't known her long. Surely, you can wait until we're all better acquainted?"

Vaughn appreciated his mother's softer stance and in any other situation, he would take her advice, but Miranda needed him *now*. Otherwise, she would lose the fortune that was due her. So he would have to spin it another way. "I'm sorry, Mom, but that's out of the question. Even though we've just met, Miranda and I are in love and we're eager to start our lives together."

His father stared at him. Vaughn wasn't in love with Miranda, but in just a few days he'd come to care for her and he was certainly attracted to her physically. *Who knew if it could develop into more?*

"That's a load of hogwash, Vaughn," his father said. "Don't try to sell me on a marriage that I know is bound to fail. I don't know the real reasons you're marrying this girl, given your claims that she has money of her own. But something is not quite right in Denver and I smell a rat! I will *not* support this lunacy."

"Enough!" Vaughn yelled. "My marriage or the reasons why are not open to a family discussion and I didn't come here for your blessing." At his words, his mother's entire face blanched and Vaughn hated that he was hurting her. "I came here because I wanted you both to know that Miranda and I are getting married this coming weekend and I'd like you both to be there. I hope you can make it."

"And your sisters?" his mother asked. "Are you going to tell them?"

"Of course, I'll contact Emily, Brianne and Eliza."

"Maybe they can talk some sense into you," his father responded hotly. "Because talking to you is like talking to a brick wall." And without another word, his father exited the living room.

Vaughn stared at his retreating back.

"Vaughn?"

"Hmm...?" He turned back to his mother, who was sitting across from him.

"Are you sure you know what you're doing?" she inquired. "This marriage is awfully sudden and I'd hate for you to make a mistake which you might come to regret later."

Was she speaking from experience, he wondered? Vaughn Ellicott, Sr. couldn't be an easy man to love or live with and they'd been together forty years. That was a long time to deal with his father's dominant ways. It was his way or the highway. That's why they'd always butted heads. Vaughn might be his namesake, but that was as far as the similarities went. They couldn't be more different. His father was tough, opinionated and regimented. Everything was black and white, but Vaughn saw things in shades of gray. It was why as soon as he'd become eighteen, he'd left home. Although the Navy was his father's old stomping grounds, Vaughn saw it as a way to see the world—and get away from his domineering father.

"I won't regret marrying Miranda," Vaughn stated. Because his marriage had a shelf life of one year which would be written into the contract. They weren't marrying for love. There wouldn't be any surprises or broken hearts if the marriage didn't work out. They would each take away what they'd brought in. Nothing more. Nothing less.

"If you're sure?" She reached across and squeezed his hand.

"I'm sure."

She smiled and nodded. "You know your father isn't going to budge. When his mind is made up, it's made up."

"I'm aware."

"Then know that though I may not agree with your decision, I'll always love you."

"Thanks, Mama." Vaughn leaned over and pulled her into his embrace, squeezing her shoulders. He understood what she wasn't saying, which was that his parents would *not* be attending his wedding.

Miranda's parents, Tucker and Leigh Jensen, took the news of her impending nuptials when she called them on the phone rather well. Miranda hadn't known what to expect when her smartphone dialed them. They weren't exactly exuberant about the news. Neither of them had been happy with the stipulation in her grandfather's will, but knew that her finding a husband was a necessary evil to keep the Jensen fortune in the family. What did excite them was the fact that Vaughn was a multimillionaire, a man who wasn't interested in taking a chunk of it.

"You're sure he doesn't want anything for agreeing to marry you?" her father inquired.

"Yes, Daddy."

"And you're getting that in writing?"

"Yes, I've already contacted the family lawyer and he's drafting the agreement now," Miranda replied, "stating that Vaughn is relinquishing any rights to my inheritance."

"Well, it sounds like it's settled," her mother replied. "I just hate that it had to come to this. I don't know why Daddy did this to you, sweetheart."

"It's not your fault, Mom. I don't blame you." And Miranda didn't. She and her grandfather had always butted heads about a woman's place. Her grandfather was old-school and felt she needed a husband and he should be head of the household and the provider.

Her mother released a long sigh. "Thank you, sweetie. I'm just worried for you. Marrying a man you hardly know."

Miranda knew enough about Vaughn and his character to make agreeing to his proposal easier. He was a man with a strong moral compass. After hearing her sob story, he could have sent her on her merry way. Instead, he'd to ask her to marry him and essentially agreed to put his love life on hold for a year. That showed Miranda that Vaughn was an upstanding guy.

"Don't worry, Mom. Vaughn is a good man. You'll see when you meet him this weekend at the wedding."

"How are you arranging a wedding in a week's time?" her mother asked incredulously. "You still have a few weeks before your thirtieth birthday."

"If it was up to me, we would go to a justice of the peace or head to Vegas for a quickie wedding and get it all over with," Miranda replied, "but Vaughn refused. With a man of his standing in the community, he wanted a proper wedding."

"But a week?"

Miranda shrugged. "I know. It seems unlikely that he can pull it off, but then again, he's rich, Mom. And when you have money, miracles can happen." Miranda looked forward to when she was independently wealthy and didn't have to rely on others. She could fulfill all her goals and dreams on her own.

"Alright, then just tell us when?" her father replied.

Miranda filled them in on all the details and her parents planned to arrive later in the week to San Diego. They would meet Vaughn before she walked down the aisle. Everything was happening so fast. Too fast. The proposal. The agreements. And now a wedding. It was hard to believe that in a week's time she and Vaughn would be husband and wife. In name only. She didn't plan on consummating their union. She couldn't. Otherwise, Miranda feared she would be caught up in the whirlwind and lose her heart to this man.

She already was acutely aware of him. Whenever he

was around, her senses were on high alert. Her blood raged in her veins while her heart would hammer loudly in her chest and her pulse would quicken. If she let him any closer, Miranda feared she'd combust. Just look at what had happened when she'd weakened and allowed Vaughn into her hotel room. She'd darn near thrown herself at him and she couldn't let that happen again.

A marriage of convenience was all she could offer Vaughn. And nothing more.

Chapter 6

"I still can't believe you're actually getting married today," Sasha said as she watched the makeup artist work on Miranda for her Sunday wedding. The hairstylist had already turned Miranda's long hair into an intricate updo with sparkly pins. Miranda could hardly believe she was almost ready to walk down the aisle to Vaughn.

In a week's time, she'd met Vaughn, he'd proposed and here they were getting married in one of San Diego's most elegant resorts, the Hotel del Coronado. When she'd flown here, she'd come on the off chance that she'd find a man willing to marry for her sizable paycheck. Instead, she'd met Vaughn, a sexy surfer and multimillionaire, who not only didn't need to marry her, but had signed away all rights to her inheritance just the day before when their lawyers had finalized their agreement. *What was he getting in return?*

A marriage to show the socialites he was off the table? Yes.

But in essence by marrying her, he was agreeing to a sexless marriage. She hadn't written it into the agreement because she hadn't wanted to be gauche. She was taking him at his word that he wouldn't try to seduce her, but Miranda wasn't just worried about Vaughn. Over the last week, he'd been nothing but a perfect gentleman, while Miranda had stewed in her own juices at her hotel room wishing she hadn't taken sex off the table. Because it was at night that her treacherous body reminded her of just how good it could be with Vaughn if she'd let go. In the morning, however, her reason would return and Miranda was glad she hadn't done something foolish like call Vaughn to extinguish the heat between her thighs.

"Are you listening to me, Miranda?" Sasha inquired, coming to stand in front of her line of vision. "You must realize how crazy this is. Marrying a man you hardly know and who couldn't even be bothered to give you his real name when you first met."

"Excuse me," Miranda said to the makeup artist as she rose to her feet and grasped Sasha by the arm. She led her into the bedroom of her suite. She'd checked in to the Hotel del Coronado a couple of days ago when her parents made it to town to meet Vaughn. The meeting had gone better than she'd expected and her parents had seemed happy with her choice of spouse. Miranda was thankful for it because she had enough to deal with, like her irate friend. "Sasha!" She glared at her friend. "You can't be spilling our secrets out there—" She pointed toward the door. "What if those women spill what they heard to the gossip rags? It could be bad for Vaughn as well as for me. The only reason he's marrying me is to stop the socialites from coming after him, not give them more fodder."

"C'mon, Miranda." Sasha folded her arms across her chest. "It has to be more than that. He has to have another agenda. I strongly urge you to reconsider this marriage."

"Sasha, you know why I have to do this." Miranda had finally broken down and told Sasha the truth because her BFF hadn't believed for a single minute that it had been love at first sight like the papers did. They had eaten up the love story and she and Vaughn had been the talk of the town all week.

"Of course I do. I know the trust fund has your hands tied, but there has to be another way. What did your lawyers say?"

"The same thing they've said for months, Sasha. This is the only way. So I need you to get behind this and stop trying to undermine my decision."

"That's not my intention." Sasha sighed. "You know I love you and I only want what's best for you, Miranda. And I worry that you're doing this—committing yourself to a marriage without love as a way to protect your heart. I know Jake and all those other men did a number on you, on your self-confidence. But you don't have to shackle yourself to this man."

"For Christ's sake, Sasha. It's a year. One year. That's all I've committed to, not the rest of my life."

Sasha threw her hands up in the air. "Okay, Miranda. It's your life. And I get that, but I wouldn't be your BFF if I didn't try to talk you out of what I believe to be a mistake. But that's it. I won't say any more."

"Thank you," Miranda said. "Now can I please get back to my makeup?"

"Of course, we have to get you beautified for your big day."

Time went by quickly when she opened the bedroom door. The makeup artist finished Miranda's face and then the photographer arrived to take getting-ready pics. Soon, Sasha and her mother were helping Miranda into her wedding dress, putting on her jewelry, shoes and handing her her bouquet.

"Let's say a quick prayer," her mother said before they left. She and Sasha circled around Miranda, placing their hands on her, and her mother prayed that their marriage would be the blessing Miranda needed and would help secure her future. Miranda was nervous as they led her out of the suite, into the elevator and through the hotel toward the beach. Onlookers were watching as Miranda made her way in her one-of-kind gown with embroidered bodice of lace and beading and stunningly full tulle skirt.

Miranda hadn't wanted a dress this grand, but Vaughn had wanted her to feel special and she did. The dress was everything she would have hoped for and loved to wear if she were getting married for real, but she wasn't. Today, she would make vows in front of Vaughn, their families, close friends and acquaintances and Miranda couldn't feel more like a fraud.

Perhaps Sasha was right. It wasn't too late to walk away. But if she did, she'd walk away from her dream of being her own boss one day. She stopped walking, startling her mother and Sasha. "You guys go ahead, okay? I just need a minute."

Sasha's brown eyes met Miranda's. She knew her better than anyone. Could she read the apprehension inside her? If she did, Sasha was remaining quiet because she had promised to be supportive for the rest of the day. And so her best friend stepped away with her mother, leaving Miranda some quiet time to think.

Miranda paced the corridor of the hotel that led to the breezeway. The beach was only a few feet away and she was sure Vaughn was standing there waiting for her in a tuxedo, probably looking fine as always. Was he as scared as she was? He certainly hadn't given her any indication. As the days had drawn near to their wedding, he'd seemed surer than ever that they'd made the right decision. *So what was holding her back?* She was benefiting the most from their arrangement.

Was it possible her feelings for Vaughn weren't as clear as they once were? Was she developing feelings for her pretend fiancé? And what did that mean for their marriage?

Miranda wrung her hands nervously together. She couldn't leave Vaughn standing out there in front of all their family and friends. She had to go through with it. But first, she should check her makeup one final time before heading to him. Where was her maid of honor? Picking up the train of her dress, Miranda started down the breezeway, but then she caught sight of Sasha and Vaughn.

They were in the breezeway having a heated discussion. Miranda slid out of the line of vision, while still allowing her to see them. *What were they talking about?* From Miranda's vantage point, Sasha was doing all the talking. Was she yet again trying to convince Vaughn to not go through with their marriage? What else could it be? She knew how strongly Sasha felt about Miranda marrying Vaughn. And when she hadn't been successful with her, she'd gone to the groom! *How could she do this?* She'd promised Miranda she would stay out of it. What if she was successful and Vaughn didn't want to go through with the wedding?

Miranda would be humiliated and she would be down to barely three weeks to find a new spouse. Tears sprang to her eyelids, but she clamped them down. No, no, no, this was not going to happen. "Sasha?" She called out her best friend's name and saw her jump away from Vaughn. "Sasha, where are you?"

"Coming," she heard Sasha say as she walked up the breezeway. Sasha was wearing a smile. *What did it mean?* "There you are. You almost saw your groom and we can't have that. It would be bad luck."

"No, we can't." Miranda couldn't read Sasha's expression. Was she putting on a good front or actually hopeful that this marriage wasn't going to be a disaster?

"Alright, let's get you over that broom." Sasha walked behind Miranda to lift her train. Miranda just hoped that when she got down the aisle, there was a groom waiting for her.

His bride had never looked lovelier than she did when she began walking toward him. Vaughn's heart constricted in his chest as Miranda glided down the aisle in a dress that was simply made for her. It hugged her every curve and revealed just a hint of cleavage before sweeping down to her hips until finally swelling out into a large train made of tulle. The look on her face as she approached him had been one of wonderment and, dare he think, happiness? *Was she surprised to find him waiting at the altar?*

He'd given his word that he would marry her, but perhaps as the seconds had ticked by, she'd begun to doubt his conviction? He hated to think so. He prided himself on being a man of honor. When he gave his word, he meant it.

And even as he said the traditional marriage vows, he meant them. For as long as Miranda was his wife, he would honor and cherish her, forsaking all others unless parted by death. And when the pastor from his family church pronounced them husband and wife and told Vaughn he could kiss his bride, he didn't give her a chaste kiss.

Vaughn kissed Miranda as if they were madly in love with one another. He cupped her face between his hands and she stared up at him in awe, then he crushed his lips to hers. His kiss was deep and passionate and he would have probed further if not for the incessant clapping in the background which told him that he'd better stop. Otherwise, they'd pass the moment of decency.

He lifted his mouth and when he did, her eyes popped open, but she didn't say a word. Instead, she allowed him to lead her down the aisle as they waved to the crowd. She was quiet as the wedding planner gave them a glass of champagne to toast their marriage. There was little time for congratulations as the photographer led them away from the cocktail hour being held on the Windsor Lawn so they could take pictures. The next hour was an arduous one for Vaughn. Thanks to the intimacy of the photographs, he and Miranda were required to kiss, touch and hold each other countless times, until Vaughn was a ball of unleashed sexual energy. He badly wanted to take Miranda back up to his room and make love to her until she cried out his name.

Instead, the planner heralded them into the reception in the hotel ballroom where they were greeted with lots of fanfare, congratulations and toasts. Together, they made their way around the room, thanking family and friends for coming. Her parents gave them best wishes, but Vaughn struggled to find them sincere. How could they allow Miranda to sell her life away? He found it hard to believe that they couldn't have figured out a way to void her grandfather's will.

They also stopped by the Millionaire Moguls' table. He'd made sure to invite a select few of the members from his organization, all of whom offered their congratulations. Christopher Marland was there and that made Vaughn uneasy. He would have thought Christopher would decline given his history with Vaughn's sister. *Had Eliza seen Christopher?* He sure hoped not; otherwise it might make for a very uncomfortable evening for her. Notably absent were Vaughn's parents, but at least Miranda got to meet his three sisters. Emily and Brianne had come with their respective spouses, while his baby sister, Eliza, had come solo.

"We're so excited to have you as part of the family." Emily, his oldest sister, pulled Miranda into a hug later that evening. "We never thought this one—" she jabbed her thumb at Vaughn "—would ever get hitched."

"Yeah, he had always been so anti-marriage, I thought we'd be old and gray before we saw the day." Brianne chuckled. "But now look at him. He's positively beaming."

Miranda glanced in his direction and something passed in her eyes that he couldn't quite name, but she smiled and said, "I'm an only child, so it's exciting to be part of a large family like the Ellicotts."

"And now our family has only gotten bigger," Eliza added.

"Thanks, sis." Vaughn squeezed her shoulders and kissed the top of her head. "You're looking lovely today, as well."

Eliza was slender, but a stunning beauty at five foot nine. Her stylishly long hair hung in soft waves down her back and she was wearing a black dress that could only be called a work of art, thanks to three tiers of ruffles along the side.

"And you, big brother—" Eliza pulled him aside from the group "—are full of surprises. You know the Commander and Mom are beside themselves at your latest stunt."

"It's not a stunt, Eliza. As you can see, Miranda and I were married for real."

"Yes, I know that," she whispered. "But why all the subterfuge? Why are we just now meeting her?"

Vaughn refused to be questioned by his little sister, no matter how well intentioned. "You met her now and that's all that matters. How are you doing, anyway? How's life in San Diego after leaving the Big Apple?" Before the ceremony had started he'd been standing at the altar, looking at the guests, and had seen Eliza looking wistful. Was she wishing her life was different? That her relationship with Marland had lasted?

"Ah." Eliza bunched her shoulders. "Certainly not as fast-paced as New York, but opening a boutique here has taken up quite a bit of my time."

"Don't work too hard."

Eliza laughed. "I believe that's your motto, not mine."

"Very funny." Vaughn grinned. "But I think it's time I finally danced with my wife. I wouldn't want her to get any ideas hanging around Emily and Brianne." He loved his two sisters, but lately they had baby fever and already had four children between them after only three and five years of marriage, respectively.

When he returned to the group, he strolled toward Miranda and circled an arm around her waist. "You don't mind if I steal my wife for a dance, do you?"

"Of course not," Emily and Brianne said almost in unison.

Vaughn led Miranda to the dance floor and hauled her soft body against his hard one. He was dying to hold her in his arms and he didn't care that the planner seemed a bit stricken as she rushed to put on their first dance selection. Eventually, the soft sounds of Kem's "Share My Life" drifted in the air and Miranda finally relaxed, expelling a short breath.

"Are you alright?" he inquired, looking down at her. "You've seemed on edge since the ceremony."

"I—I'm fine," she finally stammered. At his raised brow, she continued, "It's just all so *real*, you know? Having a wedding made it real that we're married."

"That's right, baby girl, you've hitched your train to this wagon and I'm not letting you go." Vaughn twirled her around the dance floor, causing Miranda to have to fight to keep up, but she did and when she returned to his embrace, her face was flushed with amusement.

"I didn't expect that. You're a good dancer."

Vaughn shrugged. "I learned a thing or two from all those military balls."

"Oh I just bet you did," she said, giving him a wink.

"Why don't I show you one of the things I learned," he whispered. He pressed his body into hers, grinding his hips into hers. Startled, she glanced up at him and her fingers clutched at his tuxedo jacket, but she didn't move away. Vaughn took that to mean that she knew what was coming next.

His mouth on hers.

He dipped his head until their foreheads touched and their breaths mingled as one, then he kissed her. This time his kiss was softer, gentler, but equally as potent. Their lips and tongues tangoed to a sensual tune that only the two of them could hear. Desire whooshed through him like wildfire and Vaughn knew that nothing but total consummation of their marriage was going to put it out, but he couldn't rush things. He pulled back and looked down at her. "That was nice."

"Nice?" She sounded breathless and he liked it.

"Yes. Nice. And maybe we can try later for a different adjective but for now, I think there's a cake to cut."

A large four-tier blinged-out cake with roses cascading down the side was being wheeled out to them on the dance floor that very minute. "Ready to cut the cake, Mrs. Ellicott?"

They each took hold of the gleaming gold-tipped knife handle and smiled at the camera as they cut the cake. Then, they were both piercing off a piece of cake with a fork and feeding each other. Vaughn's eyes never left Miranda's and vice versa.

It was going to be a long night.

Miranda was having a hard time separating reality from fantasy. It had been that way the entire day since she'd walked down the aisle and Vaughn had made her his wife. It had started with that amazing first kiss. She'd been expecting a quick peck on the lips, but instead, Vaughn had kissed her like their marriage was a real one. And he hadn't let up since. Throughout the reception, he hadn't strayed far from her side, constantly touching her and keeping her near him.

And again during their first dance, he'd seduced her. The way he'd held her, the world had ceased to exist and she'd wrapped her arms around him of her own accord. She hadn't stopped him when his masculine lips and talented tongue had invaded her mouth until she was a whimpering mass of need.

Need which could not be met.

She was slick between her thighs with wanting her husband and it wasn't right. She'd made the rules and she would abide by them, even if it killed her. And it damn near did.

She was happy when the evening started to draw to an end and the hotel had a dazzling fireworks display to help signal the end of the night. During the display, Vaughn procured a bottle of the finest champagne which they'd sipped under the stars. Miranda indulged, emptying the contents of the flute. Vaughn refilled it and together, they nearly polished off the bottle. Was he as anxious as she was? The day had already been spectacular, from the historic hotel on the beach, to the planner, to the world-renowned photographer, to the romantic beachside ceremony, to the elegant ballroom reception.

Vaughn had left nothing to chance. He'd arranged the wedding of her dreams. Miranda couldn't help but wish they were in love. *That* would be the icing on the cake.

Right now, they were in serious lust.

As they said their last goodbyes to his family and her parents, Vaughn grasped her hand and began leading her out of the ballroom as bubbles were blown at them.

"Where are we going?" Miranda asked, picking up her train and following him out the door.

"To the honeymoon suite, where else?"

"Honeymoon suite?" she croaked.

"Yes, where did you think we were staying?"

Miranda hadn't really thought about their wedding night beyond getting through the ceremony and reception. She'd just assumed she'd go back to her room and vice versa. "What about my stuff?"

"All taken care of. The planner had our rooms packed up and our suitcases are in the honeymoon suite."

"Oh." Her excuse was gone.

"C'mon." He led her to the elevator. Once inside, they both stood on opposite sides, staring at each other. Miranda knew what she was thinking—which was she'd like nothing better than to unzip his pants, hike up her dress and let him put her out of her misery. But instead, she did the ladylike thing, curled her arm around his and walked to the honeymoon suite.

When they reached the door, Vaughn surprised her by lifting her off her feet and carrying her over the threshold.

"Vaughn, you don't have to do this," she said as he sauntered inside the room, carrying her with little to no effort. "Nobody is watching us." He shut the door with his foot and that was when Miranda noticed that the entire suite had been decorated with all sorts of candles of various heights casting a romantic glow around the room, and rose petals were strewn across the bed.

"I did it because I wanted to." Vaughn gently placed Miranda back on her feet and, before she could speak, leaned in and kissed her.

His kiss was hot and hungry. And he plundered her mouth without restraint since this time, they had no audience. It was just the two of them alone in the room. His hands moved to her hair and his fingers impatiently wove themselves through to remove the carefully positioned pins of her updo until the strands tumbled down around her face. Miranda's heart quickened as he pulled her closer, molding her body to his until she felt the cradle of his masculinity at the apex of her thighs even through the full bodice of her dress.

"Miranda!" he whispered into her mouth and she gave a mew of pleasure that at first sounded like it was in the distance until Miranda realized it was her; she was making the moans of pleasure as he invaded her entire being.

His mouth.

His scent.

He was everywhere and she wanted him inside her. "V-Vaughn," she panted.

"Yes, baby?"

"Please…"

Reaching behind her, he began unzipping her wedding dress. And she was thankful that instead of a corset, she'd opted for ease. Had she known that the evening might end this way? Was that why she'd chosen a dress that was easy to get out off? She felt the cold air at her spine as he slowly peeled the dress off her. Using his forearm for balance, she stepped out of the concoction and stood before him in nothing but her panties and high heels.

For a moment, Vaughn just stared at her and his eyes seemed almost unseeing as he took her in. Because her wedding gown was strapless with a built-in bra, she was now half naked and so he could see her nipples had turned to bullet points.

Miranda heard his groan, seconds before his mouth drove down on hers.

Vaughn growled as powerful need—hot and consuming—tore through him. He'd waited so long—and seeing Miranda bare chested in nothing but the skimpiest of thongs undid him. He'd told himself that he would take things slowly, go at her pace, but it was impossible to do that now. Not when her glorious body was standing there and she was his for the taking.

He hauled her to him and began walking with her arms curled around his neck backward to the bed. He lowered them both, pushing aside the rose petals so his fingers could tangle in her hair as he deepened the kiss. He lost himself in her sweetness and left her delicious lips long enough to explore her face. He kissed her closed eyelids, the tip of her nose and her dimples and then his mouth grazed the curve of her jaw. He wasn't thinking about the wedding or his business or his parents' decision to not attend. There was only one thing on Vaughn's mind.

Miranda.

He wanted to seduce her.

Entice her.

She wouldn't be able to resist the attraction that ratcheted up ever since he'd walked across the beach and caught her checking him out. And now his own need, which had been battering his self-restraint, took precedence. He spread his whole body across hers and felt her full breasts push against his chest as their limbs tangled together. Then her legs clamped over his calves and she met his mouth when it came crashing down on hers. He kissed her again and again.

A groan escaped his lips as the sensation of her tongue tangling with his consumed him. "I want you," he murmured. "And you want me too?" It was a question, but he needed her assent that she too would go up in flames if they didn't come together as husband and wife.

"Yes." She whispered the word, but he heard it all the same. He cupped her jaw and angling her face, fused his mouth again with hers. He kissed her slowly and deliberately. He wanted to stir a need—because she'd been firing one in him all night. A need he couldn't name, a temptation he couldn't resist.

Miranda gave herself permission to enjoy Vaughn making love to her mouth because that was exactly what he was doing. He was luring her into his web, drawing her in and making her feel sexy. His solid frame pushed against her and her breath quickened at his hardness against her soft curves. She could feel the steel length of his arousal against her stomach and it caused an instant pulse to beat between her legs. She was awash with lust and gripped at his jacket, helping Vaughn pull it off and toss it aside.

Then she tore at his shirt until buttons popped off and went flying everywhere. She couldn't wait to touch him. When she reached skin, her hands trailed a path from his powerful shoulders to his muscled chest. Nothing had ever felt quite this good and she gloried in the feeling of his rock-hard abs as she pressed kisses to his torso and heard his sharp intake of breath when her tongue curled around one of his nipples. She circled it with her tongue, drawing the sensitive peak into her mouth until it hardened. But her exploration didn't last long.

"Later," he growled. His dark eyes gleamed with a promise of what was to come and Miranda reveled in the hunger that Vaughn evoked in her. His hands were everywhere, skimming her body. Miranda didn't shy away from his touch; instead she allowed his deft hands and sensual mouth to work wonders over every inch of her body from her throat to her earlobes, to the sensitive skin of her nape. Shivers of ecstasy coursed through her because there was no path that his hands and mouth didn't touch or taste. And when he took the weight of one of her breasts in his palm and rolled the engorged bud between his fingers, lustful pleasure welled inside her.

"Vaughn…" She let out a loud cry as wicked sensations coursed through her when he leaned in and drew the other bud into his hot, moist lips. She was so caught up in the delicious feelings he was evoking that she didn't stop him when she felt his hands trail a path down her sides to her hips and lower until he came to her entrance. Pushing the flimsy fabric of her thong aside, he slid a finger between her folds and found her hot and slick with desire for him.

"You feel so good." His voice was velvet and honey all

rolled into one and it hit Miranda in her core, causing her to clamp around his fingers. "Easy, easy." He urged her legs farther apart so he could stroke her ever so slowly.

Miranda was going to lose her mind. Vaughn was inciting her to madness. "Oh God, yes," she gasped as his fingers began to pulse faster and faster inside her.

"That's right, baby. Come for me." He increased the tempo and she greedily arched her hips for more. She craved him and his skillful fingers unlike she had any other man before him. Vaughn had just that kind of effect on her and she moved restlessly between his fingers.

And then she splintered as the entire world fell off its axis and she cried out. "Vaughn!"

He drew away from her long enough to look down at her and smooth her tousled hair from her face. "I love how responsive you are," he murmured. "And how beautiful." He bent his head to press a kiss against her lips.

As she came back down to earth after experiencing a glimpse of passion with Vaughn, Miranda's heart started and insecurity began to bubble up inside her. On the one hand, she'd felt more alive than she'd ever felt, but on the other hand if they continued down this path, it would make her feel things more deeply toward him. And that was when she knew—she shouldn't be doing this. As good as it felt, imagine what it would feel like tomorrow. She'd been here before, giving so much of herself to a man—only to have her love not be returned. If she let Vaughn make love to her, she'd get attached because he would be a part of her. And she would begin to think they had a future together when their marriage had a set end date. Men easily took women to bed and emotion didn't play a part because they were thinking with their anatomy. And much as Miranda wanted to be swept away in the fantasy of their first time together, warning bells were ringing inside her head and she began to pull away.

Vaughn recognized her reticence and pulled away to look at her. "Miranda, what's wrong?"

A bone-deep instinct told Miranda she was traversing a slippery slope, but for once she had to listen. "I'm sorry, Vaughn. I can't do this." She quickly moved away from him, sliding underneath the duvet to hide her naked body even though her entire body drummed with desire. She had to keep her distance because if she didn't, any shred of strength she had would go flying out the window if he continued to touch her.

"I don't understand." His voice was raspy with desire. "Are you honestly denying you enjoyed that?"

Words caught in her dry throat and Miranda couldn't speak. She should never have allowed the situation to get out of control. She could blame all the champagne she'd consumed but that was only part of the reason. The other part had been her. She'd wanted to feel the crush of his lips on hers and the powerful strength of his body on top of hers. "It…it's just not right, Vaughn."

"So we're debating the merits of what's right and wrong? We're married and you're my wife, for Christ's sake," Vaughn said, catapulting off the bed. The flash of emotion on his face was real and she could see anger and desire, because despite his outward appearance, he still wanted her. His body gave him away. His erection was still prominently bulging in his shorts.

"In name only," she added quietly.

"Like hell!" he roared. "You weren't thinking about a marriage in name only when you came apart in my hands just now. You were thinking about how badly you wanted me buried deep inside you."

Miranda colored at his blunt words. "I'm sorry. I screwed up. I—I was just so caught up in the moment. The wedding, our vows, the dance." She shook her head and turned into the pillows as tears began stinging her eyes. "It's all been too much."

Vaughn sighed and slowly walked over to her and scooted next to her on the bed. "Please don't cry, Miranda." He grasped her underneath her arms, forcing her to look at him. He reached out a finger and wiped the tears on her cheeks. "I'm sorry for yelling. I—I just want you so much," he growled. "And I didn't think you'd pull away. I thought you wanted me too."

"I do," she cried, lowering her lashes, "but I don't know how to do this. I don't know how to be casual about sex. Certainly not with my husband, a man I'm married to for the next year. Sex would only complicate things."

In his opinion for the better, Vaughn thought. He was sporting an enormous erection thanks to the mews of pleasure she'd made when his fingers had been buried inside her. He'd nearly come undone. "Why do you assume it would? You don't know that for sure."

"I do. I've—I've been here before. Trust me, it's safer if we don't do something rash that we might regret in the morning."

"I wouldn't regret being with you, Miranda." On the contrary, he would treasure their time together, but she didn't see it that way.

"You don't know that for sure."

"Are you looking for a one-hundred-percent guarantee that I—" Vaughn touched his chest "—or no other man will ever hurt you? Because I'm here to tell you, Miranda, that it's unrealistic. We're all human and are going to make mistakes and you can't safeguard your heart against hurt. If so, you'll miss out on passion because one thing's for certain—you have never responded to another man the way you've been with me."

"You—you can't know that." The words stammered out of her mouth.

"Oh yes I can, because I can read you, Miranda." His voice was low and husky. "I can see it in your eyes when I touch you, but you refuse to accept what's between us, so don't worry, I will leave. But I want you to think about what could have been when you're alone in the cold bed tonight." Vaughn rose to his feet. And as much as it pained him, physically as well as emotionally, he was going to have to walk away. "I'm going to go sleep on the couch."

"You don't have to do that. You could sleep here."

"I can't sleep beside you, Miranda, and not make love to you. Sleep well." He caressed her cheek and with one final glance at her trembling lips left the room and headed for the bathroom.

Once he'd shut the door, Vaughn leaned heavily against it. Stripping, he headed straight for the shower and turned on the taps as cold as he could take it and then stepped inside. He let the cold water pound on him in the hopes that it would make him less aware of his body and the raging hard-on he had which would not be assuaged tonight. He sluiced water from his face and propped his hand against the tiled wall and allowed his body to sag.

How the hell had they gotten here?

He hadn't started the day with the intent of taking Miranda to bed. He'd just wanted to give her an amazing wedding day from start to finish, from the one-of-a-kind designer gown, to the romantic beachside ceremony and the glittering reception with champagne and caviar. He'd wanted to give her the world.

Then he'd gone and mucked it all up by coming to the honeymoon suite. Vaughn squeezed his eyes shut as he recalled the memory of Miranda walking down the aisle and how stunningly beautiful she'd looked. The way her eyes sparkled from across the room throughout the night.

The way she'd felt in his arms when they'd danced. He felt so connected to her and he hadn't known he was going to feel this way.

He hadn't known that he'd feel so unrestrained toward her and that her drugging kisses would lead him to peel the wedding gown from her glorious body and start making sweet love to her. His senses had left him and her dazed expression just now told him that perhaps he had gone too far. He just hadn't known how to pull away. He'd been overtaken by an all-consuming desire to mate with her and make her his.

Wrenching off the taps, he reached for a towel to dry himself. He couldn't have predicted that she would withdraw from him, not after she'd had a spectacular orgasm by his touch. But she turned him down leaving him this sorry option to put himself to bed. When he emerged from the bathroom, he found Miranda sound asleep on the pillow with the lamp still on. Rose petals were scattered around the floor because he'd pushed them off in his haste to be with her. As he turned off the bedside lamp, there was an ache in his groin from unfulfilled sexual desire.

When he returned to the sitting room he saw Miranda's wedding dress lying in the middle of the suite. When she'd slipped out of it earlier, he'd thought they were finally about to do what came naturally between a man and a woman. But once again, she'd gotten spooked. He wanted to kill the bastard who hurt Miranda and shook her confidence and made her skittish about intimacy. He'd been astounded at just how good and right it felt to have her in his arms. Next time, he would take it slow. The next time he got a chance to be with Miranda, he'd make sure they were both completely satisfied.

Chapter 7

Miranda woke up the next morning with a throbbing in her temples. She'd drunk too much champagne at the wedding and had the headache to prove it. Slowly, she sat upright and began massaging her temples. Last night after Vaughn had walked out on her, she'd stared at the ceiling wondering if she had indeed made the wrong decision. She'd done it for her own self-preservation, but that hadn't stopped her from staying up half the night because as Vaughn predicted, she had wondered *what if.* When he'd emerged from the bathroom, she'd feigned being asleep when in fact she'd been anything but. She was buzzing with arousal and had stared endlessly at the clock until she must have eventually dozed off.

She was about to get up when the bedroom door opened and Vaughn walked in carrying a mug of what she hoped was coffee and a bottled water. "Thought you might need this," he said when he approached. He placed the mug of coffee on the nightstand and handed her the bottle. "And take a couple of these." He handed her some ibuprofen.

She went to reach for them and realized that when she'd sat up, the sheet had fallen to her waist and her breasts were completely bare to Vaughn's gaze. But instead of looking at her hungrily as he'd done the night before like he wanted to devour her, he seemed oblivious. "Thanks." She accepted the pills and watched Vaughn quickly look away.

Was he still mad at her for the abrupt end to their lovemaking? She'd done it for both their sakes. She didn't want to confuse love with sex. And that was exactly what she would have done if she'd made love to him. She knew herself. *Couldn't he see this was for the best?*

"You should shower and get dressed," Vaughn said as he moved toward the door. "I've some business to take care of today."

"Oh, that's fine, I have plenty of things to do."

"Then you'd better change your plans because you're coming with me."

Miranda stared at him, befuddled. He wanted to spend time with her after last night's debacle? She'd have thought he would be running in the opposite direction.

"I'm speaking at the *USS Midway* Museum so you need to get showered and change. So chop-chop." He clapped his hands together.

"You don't really need me there."

His brows rose a fraction. "C'mon, think, Miranda. What if the overseers of your trust found out we spent the day apart right after our wedding? What would they think? You don't want them to realize our marriage is a fake, do you? You'd lose everything."

Their marriage was fake. He'd said it aloud. And the words hung like an albatross in the air. "No, we wouldn't want that, would we?" Her voice was strained when she spoke.

"Well, then get dressed and meet me in the living room. I just called down for breakfast and it should be here any minute." Vaughn sauntered out of the room, leaving Miranda clutching the sheet and wondering how she was going to make it through the day with this frisson of sexual energy between them.

Vaughn watched Miranda as she pushed the omelet on her plate back and forth with her fork. She was no more eating her breakfast than he was this morning. All he'd managed was a cup of coffee to ensure he wasn't cranky throughout the day. He'd spent a restless and uncomfortable night on the couch when he'd much rather have been in bed with Miranda.

But she was closed off.

Afraid to allow anyone inside her heart, let alone her bed.

Vaughn wondered just how bad it must have been for her with her previous boyfriends. They must have done some number on her to keep men at arm's length. She'd certainly been doing so from the moment they met, inviting him to her room, but sending him away, sneaking out of the hotel and finally last night giving him a taste of heaven, only to pull away.

What would it take to convince Miranda he was a stand-up guy?

Time.

In time, she would see that he wasn't like the other men she'd dated. She'd find out her *husband* was so much more. Even though she was testing him. "We should leave." Vaughn stood. "The ceremony is in an hour and we don't want to be late."

"Of course." Miranda rose to her feet and followed him to the door. She glanced behind her. "Sorry about breakfast. I wasn't very hungry."

"You had a long night," he replied as he placed his hand at the small of her back, closed the suite door and guided her to the elevator bank. The elevator ride down seemed interminable with the silence between them. Vaughn was thankful when it came to an end and they reached the waiting car. After last night, he was in no mood to drive and had hired a car for the day. He opened the door and helped Miranda inside. When he joined her, she asked, "No sports car?"

"Nah, I'm a bit tired after the wedding yesterday."

"But yet you didn't cancel this appearance?"

"Why would I?" he countered. "As you've said, our marriage is one of convenience, so I'd anticipated that we would resume our normal lives, with a few minor changes of course. Plus, I'd committed to speaking at the reenlist ceremony before we met. I couldn't very go well back on my word, now could I?"

"Of course not. And I wouldn't want you to."

The awkward silence between them continued the entire ride to the *USS Midway*. When they arrived, Vaughn hoped that seeing him in a new environment might help Miranda see him differently. See that he wasn't like those other men. See that he cared for her and would never hurt her.

Miranda watched in fascination as Vaughn gave his speech onboard the floating city at sea to a group of men and women reenlisting in the United States Navy. They stood in their crisp white jumpers and hats, neckerchiefs and gleaming black shoes, staring at her husband. She'd known Vaughn had been in the Navy, but knowing and seeing him in action were entirely two different things. Even though he wasn't in military uniform like those in active duty, he looked equally stunning in a beautifully cut suit that molded to his perfect body and long legs. He stood on the podium sharing with his comrades the importance of their service and commitment to their country.

She was impressed.

Vaughn spoke with passion and conviction on how the Navy shaped him into the man he was today. As she looked around the faces in the crowd, there was nothing but admiration and respect on their faces. He'd earned it serving proudly for a decade before leaving the service. Pride swelled in Miranda's heart that he'd chosen to share this special moment with her despite the tension between them.

The ride over to the museum had been fraught with

buildup from the night before. How could it not be when she'd treated him so abominably? She should never have allowed the attraction that had been simmering beneath the surface to get that far, but she had. And because of it, she couldn't forget Vaughn. Images of his gorgeous, sexy body had assailed her throughout the tumultuous night and any hope that sleep would claim her had been darn near impossible. And even now she couldn't escape them.

His piercing eyes caught hers as he spoke and unspoken words went through time and space between them. Those unspoken words acknowledged that they would have to let go of last night if they wanted to move forward in this marriage. Miranda welcomed them because she didn't want to go back to the awkwardness of earlier that morning.

Vaughn must have sensed her surrendering the white flag because he walked toward her after the ceremony with a smile. "Well? What did you think?"

She beamed. "You were fantastic!"

He grinned unabashedly. "Fantastic. Now that's a word I like to hear. I'm glad you enjoyed it because I meant every word."

"I know you did," Miranda said. "You're a man of honor."

"I'm glad you can see that."

"I do. And for the record, that's hard for me, Vaughn. Trust doesn't come easy for me..." Her voice trailed off. "Just so much has happened in the past."

"I hear you and you won't get any pressure from me, Miranda," Vaughn said. "You've drawn a line in the sand and I'll respect that. If you wish to change it, you'll have to come over the line and make your feelings known."

Miranda nodded. If she changed her mind about their relationship, she was going to have to come to him because he wasn't going to chase after her.

"Good." He offered his hand. "Come with me then. This

museum is great and I'd love to show you around since we arrived just before the ceremony."

They spent the rest of the afternoon exploring the museum and reliving the fifty years of history of the longest active Navy aircraft carrier. They toured the flight and hangar decks and looked inside the restored aircrafts and visited the command center. Vaughn took the time to explain the inner workings of an aircraft carrier like the *USS Midway*. They talked to a former pilot who shared some interesting stories with them. She was particularly impressed when they stopped to talk with a group of schoolchildren who were there for an onboard program to help with the sciences and math. "Prescott George is doing something unique as well with our youth," Vaughn informed her.

"That's great, Vaughn. I'm sure the children appreciate the hands-on experience."

"We're looking at those who are less privileged and might benefit from the armed forces."

"Does it have to be the Navy?"

He shook his head. "It can be any branch. I don't think enough young people understand all the benefits and what programs and education are out there if they serve in the military."

"You're just the person to tell them," Miranda replied with a smile. "You're really quite captivating onstage."

"Why thank you, Mrs. Ellicott," he responded.

Hearing her new surname caused a warm tingling feeling in the pit of Miranda's stomach. Miranda was intrigued by this more regimented side of Vaughn. Since the day they'd met, she'd only seen the carefree, live-life-every-day-like-it's-your-last Vaughn, but in this setting, he was a leader in command of his surroundings. It excited her, but Miranda pushed it down, ascribing it to the whole "man in a uniform" phenomenon. Once they were off the ship, they would go back to normal.

She soon learned how wrong she was on the drive back to the hotel. "Vaughn? Where are we going?" Miranda asked peering out the window.

"Home."

"I thought we were going back to the hotel."

He quirked a brow. "What made you assume we'd be going back there?"

"Because that's where I've been staying."

"Well, your assumption is wrong because I made other plans."

"Such as?"

"My home, where else? I have plenty of room at my place by the beach. There's no need for you to stay at the hotel."

"But all my things are there…"

"Don't fret. I've had both your rooms packed up and all your belongings have been taken to my house."

Her eyes narrowed. "You had no right to do that without asking me."

"I have every right, Miranda. We're married and we should be living together. I know we married in haste and you've never seen where I live, but trust me, you will be more than comfortable."

Miranda sighed and he had a point. "I would just appreciate being consulted, Vaughn."

"I'm sorry, but you married a take-charge kind of man. I don't believe in resting on my laurels—I believe in getting the job done."

"I'll be sure and remember that."

Miranda bit her bottom lip and sulked in the backseat of the car. What right did he have to make decisions without asking her? If that was the sort of marriage he thought they were going to have, he would soon learn otherwise. She was done with being anyone's pushover. If his house wasn't acceptable, he'd be turning the car back around and eating those words.

When the car pulled up to two iron gates and they swept open, Miranda got her first view of Vaughn's place by the beach. She'd underestimated him yet again. Vaughn smiled as he helped Miranda out of the vehicle and saw her eyes widen in surprise. The property was nothing short of palatial. She loved the curvilinear design of the house that mimicked the ocean. It was white, bright and voluminous, with clean modern lines, sleek sophisticated furniture and French doors which led to a mind-blowing view of the Pacific Ocean. Vaughn showed her around the seven-bedroom, seven-bath house and Miranda's heart stopped. She could see the ocean from nearly every room.

The living room was spacious with a domed skylight and fireplace. There was a family room, a home theater and kitchen with a circular breakfast bar and freshly cut flowers. She didn't take Vaughn for the fresh flower type. It was certainly a woman's touch. A housekeeper perhaps? But it was the outdoor terrace that wrapped around the entire house that was Miranda's favorite place. She could see herself sitting outside stargazing with a glass of wine. She turned to him as she surveyed her surroundings. "You downplayed your house. Just how wealthy are you?"

He shrugged as he removed his suit jacket and ditched his tie. "I don't like to flaunt my wealth. If people choose to judge me by my appearance or the fact that I'm not dressed in a suit and tie every day, then that's on them."

"Guilty as charged." Miranda raised her hand. "Your home is stunning and I admit I misjudged you."

"Perhaps about everything?" Vaughn murmured. He was determined not to remain sulky and broody because

Miranda was choosing to keep their relationship platonic. Instead he was more determined than ever to show her that he wasn't the sort of man to run out on her.

"Let me show you the rest of the place." He walked ahead of her and punched a button.

"Is that an elevator?"

Vaughn turned to glance at her. "It is. I'm sure when they built the house, they didn't fancy we'd want to climb two flights of stairs." He inclined his head to the spiral staircase. After a short ride, the doors opened into a master suite.

"Omigod, this is even more spectacular than downstairs," Miranda said as she strolled through the sitting room, marble bath and large walk-in closet. When she came out, anxiety was written all over her face. "So the master bedroom takes up the entire third floor?"

"It does."

"I thought we agreed that this marriage would be in name only. Are you changing the rules, Vaughn?"

"Of course not. I respect your wishes. This is my room and you're free to join me here at any time."

Color stained her cheeks.

"But for the time being feel free to use any of the bedrooms downstairs. Since we're going to be husband and wife for a while, you might as well make yourself feel at home. So if you want to select different bedding or change the decor, just let me know. I can put you in touch with my interior designer. She'll work wonders for you."

"You'd do that? Even though our marriage will only be one year?"

He frowned. "You don't have to keep reminding me of our expiration date. I'm well aware of that fact."

"I'm sorry. I guess I'm just nervous. This all is happening so fast. Meeting you. The wedding. And now moving in together. I feel like I can't catch my breath."

Vaughn walked toward. "Then I suggest holding on to me." Because he was not going to stop romancing her and getting Miranda to see that he was exactly the type of man she could let go and be herself with.

Chapter 8

Miranda was nervous about what to expect living with Vaughn, but she needn't have been. Once Vaughn had given her the grand tour of his house, he disappeared to work until later that evening while she unpacked. Her suitcases had already been waiting for her in one of the spare bedrooms on the second floor. It may not be as grand as the master suite, but it held a large bedroom, private bath and balcony which was a large as some people's yards. She made quick time of unpacking her meager belongings.

She'd never thought about where she would stay after they'd gotten married. If she'd thought they'd live separately, she'd been delusional. Vaughn seemed intent on keeping her close by. Miranda had to admit she liked the attention and was a bit forlorn when she found a few hours had passed without any sign of Vaughn. So she went in search of him.

She'd hadn't realized he was so driven. She'd thought he worked occasionally when the mood suited him, but she couldn't have been further from the truth. Vaughn was dedicated to his company and his employees.

She found him in his office with a view of the sun setting over the ocean. He was on speakerphone and advising Kindra to ensure everyone in the office got a bonus due to a contract Elite just landed.

She'd known that he cared about the people who worked for him because he'd told her about the healthy program he offered at work with the fitness center, organic lunch delivery and standing work stations, but to hear him in his own words was astounding. She also was shocked to find his office neat and tidy. She'd never imagined him to be so rigid. Perhaps it came from all his time in the Navy. There wasn't a stitch of paper on his modern circular desk that was similar to the house's design. It held two monitors and a wireless keyboard.

She was wondering how he managed to work without paper when Vaughn turned around and caught her checking out his office. He smiled.

"I'm going to have to let you go," he said into the mouthpiece. "My wife has arrived." Seconds later, he clicked the headpiece on his ear and whipped it off, setting in on the desk. "Don't stand in the doorway. Come in."

Slowly, Miranda walked inside and came forward. She stroked the side of his desk. "This is nice. Was it intentional?"

"You mean the shape?" At her nod, he said, "Yes, it was. As soon as I saw this house, I fell in love. It fit my personality since I love the sea so much."

She leaned against the side of the desk, facing him. "Yes, it does. I couldn't help but overhear your conversation. Do you always reward your employees so grandly?"

He shrugged. "When I can. Business is good and if I reward hard work, I'll have loyal employees."

"Good tactic."

"I find that the slow and steady approach in life usually works best." Vaughn regarded her intensely.

Miranda wasn't sure she liked his steady gaze boring into hers. It made her uncomfortable. She shifted from foot to foot. "Well, uh, I was just wondering if you were getting hungry." At the mention of food, her stomach growled, letting her know that it had been hours since she'd eaten. They'd pretty much gone from the reenlistment ceremony into touring the aircraft carrier without breaking for lunch. She'd been so enthralled, food hadn't occurred to her until now.

Vaughn chuckled. "It appears I've been remiss in my duties as a husband. Come." He took her hand. "Let's get you fed."

They stopped in their rooms to change clothes, and then Vaughn uncorked a delicious red wine for Miranda to drink before laying steaks on the grill on the terrace. In yoga pants and a tank top, Miranda curled her legs underneath her on a chaise and sipped on the excellent vintage as she watched a master at work. Miranda couldn't recall ever being treated so divinely.

"Who taught you how to cook?" she inquired after he'd turned the seasoned steaks on the grill. She couldn't picture his father, the Commander, in the kitchen. "Was it your mother? Or maybe your granny?"

With tongs in hand, he turned to face her. "Neither. I taught myself."

"You did?"

"Don't sound so shocked. When you're on a Navy ship, there's not much else to do with your time off. I used to go in the kitchen and watch the cooks. And I asked a lot of questions."

Miranda liked how down-to-earth and approachable Vaughn was. Even though he was a wealthy man, he seemed really in tune with himself and others around him. She envied him that. Sometimes she wondered if she ever really knew herself. It wasn't until recently when she'd begun to dream of her bed-and-breakfast that she realized she wasn't just a rich man's granddaughter.

"So what are you making to accompany that divine piece of meat?" The aromas wafting from the grill were tempting her tummy.

"I'm not really into carbs," Vaughn said, and patted his

flat stomach. "So I thought I'd toss up a salad if that's al-right with you?"

"Works for me."

"Excellent. I'm here to serve you." Vaughn bowed on his way back into the house toward the kitchen. She would love to have him serve her in a number of different ways and positions. A blush immediately bloomed across Miranda's cheeks. Where had that come from? *And did Vaughn know just how far her thoughts had gone?*

He returned several minutes later carrying a colander with mixed greens and a bottle of vinaigrette dressing and table settings for two.

"Let me help you." Miranda began to rise but he shook his head.

"Absolutely not. Enjoy your wine. And your dinner will be served shortly."

He set the table on the patio, returned to the grill and removed the steaks, setting them on a platter to rest. Then he returned to the kitchen and brought back the bottle of red, topping off Miranda's and pouring himself a glass. "Come on over." Vaughn motioned her over to the table.

Miranda inhaled the aroma. "Looks delicious," she commented as she sat down.

Soon Vaughn was serving her steak and salad and toast-ing to them. "To our first night together as husband and wife."

She chuckled. "Ummm… I think that was last night."

"Our first night in our home then," he responded, hold-ing up his glass. "Salut."

"Salut." Miranda sipped her wine and looked across the table at Vaughn. He looked devastatingly handsome even though he was wearing drawstring shorts and a wife-beater. But to Miranda he'd never looked sexier, except maybe in that wet suit on the beach.

"You know I have to eventually go back to Chicago," Miranda ventured. He'd called this place their home.

Vaughn frowned. Why did she always have to remind them of their arrangement? "This *is* your home now," he stated. "And you will live here with me."

She plunked her wineglass down. "Is that an order, because I don't respond well to being bossed around."

"No, it's merely a fact that I don't intend on having a long-distance marriage. That's not part of this deal."

"Vaughn, we never discussed living arrangements. And my job is back in Chicago."

"So you merely expected to marry a stranger and resume your normal life?"

"It was going to be a business deal."

"It is, but one of the reasons that marrying you appealed to me—" other than the fact she was hotter than sin "—was that I needed a spouse to keep my parents off my back and to keep other women at bay. I can't do that if you're in Chicago full-time. And didn't you say you might want to open up a bed-and-breakfast here?"

She pursed her lips. "I did."

"And now that you'll have access to your inheritance, you can make that dream a reality. I can help you."

"You would?"

"Of course. You're my wife." She stared at him in bewilderment, so he added, "Plus, in case you need a reminder I know a little something about launching a successful business."

"Yes, I suppose you do."

"So tell me about more about your idea."

Vaughn listened as Mariah shared her thoughts on her B and B. They talked well into the night, eventually retiring inside to clean up their dinner dishes and head to bed.

As he walked Miranda to her bedroom, Vaughn hated

that they were sleeping separately especially when it was clear that Miranda wanted to be with him. Patience had never been his virtue. He was a man of action and believed in going after what he wanted, but in this instance his bull-doggedness would not get him in Miranda's bed. Instead, he would have to show her day in and day out that he was worth taking a risk on.

It surprised Vaughn how much he wanted to earn Miranda's respect. He wanted her to trust him while in his other relationships he'd never cared one way or the other. Why? Because they'd never meant as much to him as the long-haired beauty. Somehow, she'd quietly worked her way into a special place in his heart. And that scared him.

The next few days were some of the best Miranda could ever recall spending in the opposite sex's company. Vaughn was good-natured and easygoing and it made living with him a breeze. Miranda wondered if he was like this with every woman or just her. After their first spat, he'd made sure to include her in his plans or share his schedule. And Vaughn had a busy one. If he wasn't at the office, at a Prescott George meeting or surfing the waves, he was with Miranda, showing her the city and taking her downtown to the Gaslamp Quarter or to Old Town and Little Italy.

Other times, even though he had an early morning, he would wake up and have a hot cup of coffee waiting for her or fix her a breakfast of veggie omelet, whole wheat toast and fresh fruit. He was making it hard for Miranda to think about ever leaving. She was scared at how often she thought about Vaughn. He hadn't so much as made a move toward her in days and it was driving her crazy. By not touching her, kissing her, he was making her want him. Was that his endgame? It had to be. Because inevitably when she couldn't bear it anymore, she would come to him. But if she did, Miranda was sure she'd lose her heart to Vaughn. If she hadn't lost it already.

One day he surprised her and took her sailing and told her they were going to fish. Miranda was a city girl and had never fished a day in her life. "You're full of surprises. Is there anything you don't do?"

Vaughn regarded her. "Not much."

"Who taught you how to sail?" Miranda inquired as she watched Vaughn bait a fishing pole and throw his line in the water.

"The Commander. He loves the sea as much as I do. The only reason he came ashore was because he felt it was time to settle down and start a family."

"Is that when he met your mother? Was it love at first sight?" Miranda had always been a romantic at heart.

He looked at her a long time. "No, it wasn't a love match. My father was a pragmatist. He found a loyal, God-fearing woman with good morals and values from a solid family. And I think my mother was looking to get away from her father's grasp only to find herself married to the Commander."

"If it wasn't a love match, why do you think your mother stayed?"

"Don't get me wrong. I think she's grown to love him in her own way, but he isn't an easy man to love."

"That sounds grim," Miranda replied. Even though she'd married Vaughn with no illusions that they were marrying for love, Miranda had always felt that when she married *for* real, it would be for love. "I hear some animosity toward your father. I thought he's been a mentor to you. Was I wrong?"

"He has been a mentor. He lives his life by a strong set of values and code of ethics which I admire and try to adhere to," Vaughn responded and stared off into the distance.

"Is your parents' marriage the reason why you've remained single for so long? Have you never found anyone worth getting serious about?"

"I've remained single because the right woman has not come along to pique my interest."

"So you've attached yourself to me because you think you'll have peace for the next year?" The more time she spent with Vaughn, the deeper insight she was getting into the type of man he was, and she liked everything she saw.

"I doubt that," he mumbled underneath his breath.

"What was that?"

"Nothing. We've arrived at our destination. We should disembark."

He anchored the boat close to a small pier and helped lift Miranda up to the dock. It felt good to be in his arms if only for a moment. Once he'd climbed over, they walked hand-in-hand to the beach. Miranda was starting to get comfortable with Vaughn's insistence that they act like a normal couple and hold hands. She doubted anyone was watching, but she acquiesced.

When he found a good spot on the beach, he pitched an umbrella in the sand and spread out a blanket. She watched him deftly prepare not only the fish he'd caught, but lay out a feast from a picnic basket he'd procured from the bottom of the boat. "When did you find time to do all this?" she inquired as she pulled off her cover-up and revealed the bikini she'd been wearing underneath.

He shrugged. "I had a little help." But when he turned to face her and caught sight of her in her bikini, there was no denying the passion in his eyes.

Miranda had to admit she felt a warm rush of heat travel up her spine, but she pushed it down. And instead, enjoyed the sunlight, fish, wine and all the accompaniments that Vaughn had brought along, which included a broad selection of sliced meats, cheeses and fruits. When she'd filled her belly, Miranda laid out on a blanket and thought about what a glorious day they'd shared together.

"You know if you want, you can take full advantage of the seclusion of the beach and sunbathe."

"Go topless?" Miranda inquired, pulling down her sunglasses to peer him.

"Sure. Why not?"

"B-because…"

"Because of what?" He quirked a brow. "Are you scared to live a little dangerously? C'mon, Miranda. You can't be afraid to live. No one is here but you and me."

She knew that. And that was exactly the problem. Even though he'd seen her naked, she was still self-conscious.

"Will it help if I turn away?" Vaughn inquired. He turned his back to her and faced the opposite direction. "Now go ahead and lose the top."

"Are you daring me?"

"If the shoe fits." She heard rather than saw the smile in his voice. He was right. What could it hurt? Reaching behind her, she caught the two strings knotted at her neck and loosened them until her top fell in her lap. Then she lay down on her stomach and said, "You can turn around now."

Vaughn spun around to find Miranda lying face down on the blanket with her plump, round bottom directly in his line of vision. Her itty-bitty bikini top was by her side. Had he really convinced her to discard it? He hadn't actually thought she'd do it, but he was glad she had. It showed him that she was becoming more relaxed in his company. "Would you like me to put some sunblock on your back?"

She turned her head and gave him a sideward glance. "Please. It's in my beach bag."

Vaughn reached inside her bag and procured the lotion and rubbed some in his palms. Then he scooted over until his knees touched Miranda and placed his palms on her back between her shoulder blades. He loved the feel of her soft and delicate skin in contrast to his roughness. As he rubbed his hands all over her, she warmed under his touch. Was she as turned on by this act as he was? It appeared to be because she began to fidget underneath him.

"Th-that's good," she whispered. "Thanks."

"Anytime." But he didn't mean it. Not if he couldn't do more than just touch her. He wanted to taste her. Kiss her. Lick her all over. She was driving him crazy with lust. Jumping to his feet, Vaughn tossed his T-shirt over his head, shoved his shorts down until he was in his swim trunks and made a mad dash for the ocean.

He was in desperate need of cooling off.

He was an excellent swimmer and took full advantage of the sea to deliver some much-needed relief. He'd been doing his best to make Miranda feel welcome in his home. In the hopes that eventually, she'd make her way to his bed. But she was proving to be a lot more stubborn than he thought. She had to be just as miserable as he was, denying what was so clearly obvious.

They wanted each other.

Night after night. They sat talking endlessly, playing chess, and watching television, anything to stave off what they really wanted to do which was to be in each other's arms. For example, right now he should be stripping off her bikini bottom, discarding his own and taking her right there on the beach in the sun, sand and surf. Instead, he was trying to exhaust himself by swimming furiously in the ocean.

Once he felt suitably tired, Vaughn headed ashore. When he arrived, he found Miranda had spun around onto her back. Her beautiful round globes were jutting forward toward the sun, the chocolate nipples hardened enough for him to lick, and Vaughn stopped dead in his tracks.

As if sensing him, Miranda jerked upright. Neither

Dear Reader,

IT'S A FACT: if you answer 4 quick questions, we'll send you **4 FREE REWARDS!**

I'm not kidding you. As a leading publisher of women's fiction, we value your opinions... and your time. That's why we are prepared to **reward** you handsomely for completing our mini-survey. In fact, we have 4 Free Rewards for you, including 2 free books and 2 free gifts.

As you may have guessed, that's why our mini-survey is called **"4 for 4".** Answer 4 questions and get 4 Free Rewards. It's that simple!

Thank you for participating in our survey,

Pam Powers

To get your 4 FREE REWARDS:
Complete the survey below and return the insert today to receive 2 FREE BOOKS and 2 FREE GIFTS guaranteed!

"4 for 4" MINI-SURVEY

1 Is reading one of your favorite hobbies?
☐ YES ☐ NO

2 Do you prefer to read instead of watch TV?
☐ YES ☐ NO

3 Do you read newspapers and magazines?
☐ YES ☐ NO

4 Do you enjoy trying new book series with FREE BOOKS?
☐ YES ☐ NO

YES! I have completed the above Mini-Survey. Please send me my 4 FREE REWARDS (worth over $20 retail). I understand that I am under no obligation to buy anything, as explained on the back of this card.

168/368 XDL GMYK

FIRST NAME

LAST NAME

ADDRESS

APT.#

CITY

STATE/PROV.

ZIP/POSTAL CODE

Offer limited to one per household and not applicable to series that subscriber is currently receiving.
Your Privacy—The Reader Service is committed to protecting your privacy. Our Privacy Policy is available online at www.ReaderService.com or upon request from the Reader Service. We make a portion of our mailing list available to reputable third parties that offer products we believe may interest you. If you prefer that we not exchange your name with third parties, or if you wish to clarify or modify your communication preferences, please visit us at www.ReaderService.com/consumerschoice or write to us at Reader Service Preference Service, P.O. Box 9062, Buffalo, NY 14240-9062. Include your complete name and address.   K-218-MS17

READER SERVICE—Here's how it works:

of them spoke a word. They both seemed entranced as Vaughn looked at her face and then at her breasts and then back up again. Only then did Miranda clutch the magazine she'd been reading across her bare bosom. "I'm sorry. I—I didn't realize you'd returned. I was just…"

Vaughn shook his head. "No need to apologize, Miranda. This is a secluded beach and you're my wife who just so happens to have the most beautiful breasts I've ever seen."

Her cheeks flamed and he could see he'd embarrassed her. "It was a compliment." She reached for her bikini top and fumbled trying to put it on while holding the magazine in place.

Vaughn walked over, kneeled beside her and took the strings from her trembling fingers. She securely held the top to her bosom while he tied the knot at her nape and her back. "Feel better now?" he whispered in her ear. Not that she could stop him from fantasizing and remembering how lush her breasts looked and how he'd tasted them once.

"Vaughn?"

"Hmm…?"

"I asked if you were ready to head back."

"Oh yes of course," he said. "Let's do it." They packed up the blanket, remaining food items and empty wine bottle and headed back to the boat. As they sailed away from the beach, Vaughn wondered just how long Miranda was going to continue this farce because it was just a matter of *when* they became lovers, not *if.*

Chapter 9

One day seamlessly rolled into another. Miranda found a real estate agent to search for the perfect property in Malibu for her bed-and-breakfast. Meanwhile, she started working on her business plan. Although she'd be using a portion of her inheritance to start the bed-and-breakfast, she planned on getting bank financing for the rest. As she'd told Vaughn, she wanted to help those less fortunate just like Prescott George.

When they weren't at work, they were at the beach. Vaughn was clearly in love with the sea. "Now that I've initiated you into sunbathing topless, I think it's only fair you learn how to water-ski and windsurf," he told her that weekend.

"I don't much like water sports."

"That's because you're afraid," Vaughn said. "I will teach you how not to be."

Much to her chagrin, Vaughn didn't drop the subject and over the course of the next week, she found him to be a remarkably patient teacher. He would pick her up in his Porsche and take her to the beach. She couldn't help the leap of excitement that surged through her tummy at spending time alone with him. She'd come to trust Vaughn because he would never let anything happen to her.

She wasn't the best swimmer, but Vaughn seemed determined her fledgling skills would improve. And under his careful guidance, she did. He had boards set up for their use. A brand-new shiny one with lots of flowers on it and a black one that looked worn and used. He made sure to show her how to wax the surfboard and paddle on her stomach until she was comfortable in the aqua blue waters of the Pacific. Miranda liked that Vaughn was sharing this part of himself with her. With a man as brilliant and powerful as he was, surfing was a way for him to relax and get away from the pressures of life. And he was giving her insight into his happy place.

Of course, there were spills and wipe-outs, but eventually she became more confident in her swimming. Consequently, Vaughn got her to attempt water-skiing and windsurfing. She didn't much like being behind the speedboat but with Vaughn at her side, giving her verbal cues and smiles, she found herself improving. She was no master. Not by a long shot, but thanks to Vaughn, she'd become carefree and was making discoveries all the time about what she was and was not capable of doing.

A couple of days later, as Miranda was knee-deep in facts and figures, Vaughn came in the house to find her working at the dining room table on Friday afternoon. He'd told her that she could change one of the spare bedrooms into an office, but Miranda had been hesitant to make any sweeping changes to the house because she knew she was only a temporary occupant. But that didn't stop her from wondering: What if things were different?

What if they had a *real marriage*? A marriage that had nothing to do with money or wills. A marriage that had only to do with the two of them loving each other. With a man like Vaughn, Miranda knew it was possible, but she couldn't allow herself to go there. What purpose would it serve? She'd already made her bed and now she had to lie in it.

"Ready to take a break?" he asked.

She looked up and saw that he was dressed like he'd just come from the office, in tailored slacks and black buttondown shirt. It never ceased to amaze her the effect he had on her with his broad shoulders and powerful build. Her skin tingled and a fire burned from the inside out just from his strong, male presence.

"Yes, I'd love one. What did you have in mind?" She didn't care if he was cooking for her or they were going out to eat, because whenever she was in Vaughn's company she had a good time, felt giddy even. And she hadn't felt this way about any of the man she'd met before. In comparison, they'd been schoolgirl crushes to what she felt when she was around Vaughn.

When she was with Vaughn, she felt like a woman. A woman who was quickly becoming unnerved just by being near him. He commanded her attention and more and more was bending her to his will. Forcing her to see that there was no way she could continue being celibate in this marriage, with *this man*.

Her man.

"Miranda?"

"Yes?"

"I'm taking my wife out for an exclusive dinner." From behind his back, he pulled out a large wrapped gift box. "Something special for you to wear tonight. So head upstairs to get dressed and I'll meet you down here in a half hour."

That didn't give Miranda a whole lot of time, but she didn't care. She wanted to spend time with Vaughn. He had a way of putting her at ease. From the way he talked to her. Looked at her. Even smiled at her. From the beginning, he'd made her feel special. After her past heartaches, she'd told herself that she didn't need anyone anymore.

But she was starting to need Vaughn.

Miranda excitedly tore the wrapping paper off the box and pulled out a beautiful beaded spaghetti slip dress with a plunging bodice that was sure to show the swell of her breasts and an empire waist before shirring out-ward. She couldn't wait to put it on. She showered with a fragrant body wash and toweled herself dry. Then added the matching lotion that held a hint of sheen to give her skin a burnished glow. She wrapped the towel around her bosom while she added a touch of powder to her face, sooty mascara to her lashes and peach lip gloss to her lips. She wanted to look beautiful, yet natural. Tossing the towel aside, Miranda eased into the dress, foregoing a bra. The dress had built-in support, so she wouldn't need it.

It was a perfect fit and would show plenty of leg due to the strappy sandals that had been included in the box along with a beaded cocktail purse. She spritzed perfume at her wrists, earlobes and at her bosom. Then she looked at the woman standing in the mirror. It was her alright, but there was something else. Her eyes were bright. Excite-ment was coursing through them at the idea of spending the night with her thoughtful husband.

She found him downstairs waiting for her in a black din-ner jacket, crisp white shirt opened at the nape and tailored trousers. He looked every bit the Millionaire Mogul the ladies of San Diego lusted after and she was one of them. She *wanted* her husband.

Miranda was a sight for sore eyes, Vaughn thought as she walked toward him. She looked hot in the dress he'd chosen for her as he'd known she would. He held his hand out to her and she came willingly. "You look stunning."

She flushed and color stained her cheeks. "Thank you."

"You ready to go?"

"Yes, but where are we going?" she inquired as he walked her toward the door.

"A restaurant, but I don't believe it has a name."

The drive to the restaurant was a half-hour drive from La Jolla so Vaughn caught up with Miranda on her day and she informed him on how progress with her bed-and-breakfast was going. He liked that she opened up to him. That over the last couple of weeks, they'd grown closer, talking late into the night. He liked that she could give him a look from across the room and he could tell what she was thinking, feeling.

Miranda wasn't able to hide her feelings from him which was why he knew that *tonight* something had changed. He'd sensed it the moment she'd come downstairs looking like an angel.

His angel.

It was in her eyes that she'd made a decision. He hoped it was what they'd been working toward the last couple of weeks. Trust in each other. He knew it wasn't easy for her given the men who'd hurt her in the past, but he wasn't those men. He'd never hurt Miranda and wanted a clean slate. And tonight after many long sleepless nights, it seemed she just might be able to give him one.

They arrived at an estate a short while later. Vaughn pressed the window down and, after speaking into the buzzer, the black iron gates parted and he drove up a short winding path to a two-story house on a high cliff overlooking the ocean.

Miranda turned to him with a puzzled expression. "This doesn't look like a restaurant. It's someone's home. What's going on?"

Vaughn grinned as he turned off the engine. "It's a surprise." He walked around to the passenger side and helped Miranda out of the car. He encircled his arm around hers and led her to the entrance. He pressed the doorbell and a uniformed butler greeted them at the door.

"Mr. and Mrs. Ellicott, please come in."

Miranda gave him a questioning sideward glance, but didn't say anything. Instead, she allowed the butler and

Vaughn to lead her to the great room where several other couples were already in attendance.

"Vaughn!" A Frenchman in a white chef coat came toward him. "So glad you and your wife could make it."

"Wouldn't miss one of your dinner parties," Vaughn said. "Chef Jean, this is my beautiful wife, Miranda."

"Elle est belle!" Chef Jean lowered his head to kiss the back of Miranda's hand. "She is lovely, Vaughn. You are a lucky man."

"Don't I know it?"

Chef Jean walked them around the room, introducing his A-list of guests: a Hollywood super couple whose new movie was making millions at the box office; a Senatorial hopeful from an old money family hoping he was a shoo-in; then he saw contemporary artist Jordan Jace and his woman of the week. The man was known for loving and leaving them. Six feet two, Jordan was long-limbed with a slender frame and his signature goatee. In his usual hipster style, he was wearing jeans, a vintage tee and a blazer.

"Jordan Jace, I'd like you to meet my wife. Miranda, I'd like you to meet Jordan Jace. Jordan is a fellow board member of Prescott George, albeit a reluctant one, isn't that right?"

"Your wife?" Jordan stared back at Vaughn like he was crazy.

"Yes, that's right. Perhaps if you'd come to meetings once in a while you'd know that."

"Couldn't be helped," Jordan responded evenly and turned to Miranda. "It's a pleasure to meet you. I can't believe you ensnared San Diego's most eligible bachelor and brought Vaughn to his knees."

Miranda stared in awe at both men. She had no idea that Vaughn rubbed elbows with such rich and famous people, especially an artist of Jordan's caliber. She'd been following his rise to fame the last several years. He was brilliant. Miranda was completely out of her element, but managed to answer Jordan. "I don't think anyone can ensnare Vaughn unless he wants to be." She turned to her husband at her side. "Isn't that right, darling?"

"Of course, my love." Vaughn placed a kiss on her forehead.

"Well, then, I'm sorry I missed the love story and the wedding," Jordan responded. "Do tell." He grabbed Miranda's arm and led her away from Vaughn, much to his chagrin.

Miranda was amused. Jordan was quite funny and she didn't mind his outgoing nature. He spoke his mind and she appreciated that.

"How did you meet Vaughn?"

"At the beach."

Jordan rolled his eyes. "Of course, what was I thinking? And was it love at first sight?"

Lust was more like it, but Miranda chuckled. "Yes, something like that." Or at least that was the spin they were telling everyone.

"Considering Vaughn's reputation with the ladies, it's great that you can put that aside and focus on your relationship."

"Were there that many?" Miranda inquired. From her research she'd seen that he dated, but he'd been a single man after all. She had no right to get jealous about women he had been with before her. Their marriage was fake, but if she was honest Miranda wanted Vaughn solely focused on her.

"It's not for me to say—" Jordan touched his chest "—but you should know that he gets around, but then again so do I."

As if he was thinking about her, Vaughn motioned her away from Jordan and over to the couple he was speaking with. He didn't look particularly pleased when he handed her a glass of champagne, but he didn't say anything. He kept his arm firmly around her while the group chatted for much of the cocktail hour while eating the sumptuous feast Chef Jean had laid out. There was a raw bar with oysters, crab claws, large prawns and an imported cheese station for guests to enjoy at their leisure. Uniformed waiters served hot hors d'oeuvres of lobster and shrimp empanadas, citrus-marinated bacon-wrapped scallops, mini beef Wellingtons with béarnaise sauce and fig and goat cheese flatbreads. They indulged in all the yummy food and Vaughn made sure to hold her hand on the way to the formal dining room.

To ease the tension between them, she said, "Jordan is an interesting character."

"Yeah, he is," Vaughn replied as they walked into the grand room. "He was one of the newer members to Prescott George and not easily led."

"I can see that. He dances to the beat of his own drum."

"Yes, he does."

She noted the note of derision in Vaughn's tone. "He's an artist."

"That may be so, but he has a role in the organization same as us. I just wish he was as passionate as the rest of us."

"Try getting to know him. You might be surprised how he opens up."

Vaughn turned to stare at her. "You might be right."

He helped her into the seat which held a place card with her name and moved to sit across from her. Several times throughout the night Miranda caught Vaughn staring at her from across the table. She was sure Chef Jean had strategically sat them as newlyweds away from each other to ensure they mingled with the other guests. Miranda found herself next to Jordan and he was great company. He was funny and outgoing.

"I find it hard to believe that Vaughn was able to keep you under wraps for so long," Jordan said from her side when the first course of the four-course dinner menu came out.

She laughed. "It's not like he had me locked up in a tower." She sipped on the signature wine pairing that came with the course.

"True, but Vaughn has always been a straight shooter, the sort of guy that what you see is what you get. Who knew he was so mysterious?" Jordan wondered aloud.

Miranda had to admit he was right. At first blush, you might think Vaughn was a surfer dude or that he might be a straight and narrow military guy, but you'd be wrong. Yes, he was disciplined when it came to his work ethic and Prescott George. He had no time for foolishness, but then he was easygoing and carefree when he was on the water. She loved watching him surf and become one with the sea, soaring through the water. She doubted she'd ever be as good a surfer as he was no matter how much he tried to teach her.

"He's not the only mysterious man in the room." Miranda turned the tables. "What makes an eccentric artist such as yourself join an organization like Prescott George?"

"I haven't been a member long."

"Why become a member at all?"

"My father's a member in London and my family hasn't necessarily championed my career despite my success, so I was throwing them a bone, if you will," he said with a grin.

"That's very generous of you, but something tells me you're only humoring them."

Jordan shrugged. "What can I say?"

As each course was served, Miranda found it difficult

to focus because every time she glanced up she found Vaughn's eyes on her following her every move. To cover her nervousness, Miranda indulged in each new wine that was offered.

"You both are so sweet, you're giving me a toothache," Jordan commented from her side when he caught their furtive glances. "It's clear how besotted you both are."

Besotted?

Miranda knew that her feelings for Vaughn had blossomed from like to lust and more. She was falling for the handsome surfer and apparently it was evident to everyone in the room because Jordan wasn't the only one who mentioned it.

"I remember what it was like to be in love," Chef Jean commented during the third course and looked over at his partner of fifteen years.

Miranda had blushed, but Vaughn hadn't. He'd seemed proud that she was the woman on his arm. She'd never felt this secure in her previous relationships. Was it because Vaughn didn't want anything from her, but *her*? What would it be like if she allowed herself to give in to the simmering passion between them? Would she survive it?

A lump formed in Miranda's throat as she nervously looked over at Vaughn while dessert was served. It was a spread of small bites that melted in your mouth, but Miranda could hardly taste it. How could she when Vaughn wasn't hiding the naked hunger in his eyes every time those gorgeous dark brown eyes peered at her. But did he smile like that at every woman? Jordan had mentioned Vaughn's reputation and so had Sasha.

When the evening came to a close, Vaughn slid his arm around Miranda's waist as they said their goodbyes to Chef Jean, Jordan and his date and the other couples. It had been a wonderful evening despite her anxiety over what might happen when they got home.

* * *

"Everything alright?" Vaughn inquired once they made it back to his estate. "You were quiet for most of the ride home." Usually they shared a great rapport, but tonight he'd caught her covert stares beneath long mascara-coated lashes. Her awareness of him had grown as the meal had progressed even though she'd attempted to hide it. He was glad when the evening ended.

"It's nothing." Miranda threw her clutch purse on the table by the front door.

Vaughn grasped her shoulder and turned her around to face him. "Don't say it's nothing when something is clearly bothering you. Just talk to me."

When he released her, she folded her arms across her chest. "How many girlfriends have you had?"

"Excuse me?"

"I'd like to know how many you've had. Jordan indicated that there's quite a laundry list."

Vaughn scowled. "Jordan had no right to speak about my affairs which are none of his business." He started toward the living room and went straight to the wet bar. He didn't appreciate being questioned about his past when it had nothing to do with them and their burgeoning relationship. He'd tried to be the best man he could be and still it wasn't enough.

"Is that what they were? Affairs?" She followed him into the room, her heels clicking on the marble floor.

Vaughn counted to ten as he poured himself a drink. He'd been on edge half the night, watching Miranda laugh and talk with Jordan while he was marooned with the boring A-list actress who couldn't stop talking about her next movie. Meanwhile his wife appeared a little too friendly with Jace, in his opinion.

"If you're asking me if I lived like a monk, I didn't. There were women, Miranda, but I was never serious about any of them." He turned to her to see her reaction. "Does that help?"

She nodded, casting her eyes downward. "Yes."

"And you? I know there had to be someone special because I've been paying for their mistakes."

When she glanced up, her expression was crestfallen and Vaughn hated himself for bringing it up, but he had to if they were going to get past it. "Any man who didn't want you, Miranda, or didn't know what he had with you was a fool."

Tears clouded her eyes and he couldn't stand the vulnerability he saw on her face. He placed his tumbler on the cocktail table, went toward her, lowered his head and brushed his lips softly across hers. He didn't want to alarm her, but all the air in the room was whooshing out of his lungs and only Miranda could fill the vacuum it left behind. So he kissed her again, moving his lips more solidly overs hers.

"Don't do this, Vaughn," she whispered when the cool tip of his tongue met her parting lips.

"I can't help myself," he murmured, stroking his tongue with hers as the taste of her filled his mouth, "and neither can you." His control was slipping, had been for weeks because she'd stirred a need that could no longer be denied. The silk and cloth between them was a hindrance because he hungered for her and she needed to feel exactly what she was doing to him.

Vaughn pulled Miranda into his arms. She went to him this time, unresisting and eager for the passion she knew was waiting there. He cradled her jaw in his hand, lifted her face until it met his and kissed her harder. And this time, some of the tension bunched up in her shoulders slowly began to unwind.

"I've been thinking about kissing you all night long. Thinking about doing this." His lips moved from her lips and trailed a path of light kisses to the curve of her throat. "Kissing you here. Touching you." His hands splayed out so he could bring her backside closer to him and she could feel the firm ridge of his arousal against her middle.

He possessively moved his hands across her breasts, encountering the rock-hard tips of her nipples. He felt her tremble wildly underneath his featherlight touch. He couldn't wait to taste them and without waiting for any invitation, he slid one of the slender straps of her spaghetti strap dress down her shoulders. He kissed the soft skin of her shoulder and allowed his mouth and lips to travel lower. Pushing the fabric aside, he was happy to find her naked underneath. His mouth closed around the hard peak of one nipple and sucked.

"Oh!" Miranda's gasp was soft, but she didn't ask him to stop. He continued laving it with quick flicks of his tongue, moistening the nub before pushing down the other strap until her bosom was completely bare and he could pay the other equal homage. Miranda fell backward, but Vaughn kept a palm firmly nestled in the small of her back as he held her in his arms, making love to her breasts.

Vaughn, however, was greedy. He wanted more. "Please tell me you want this?" The urgency in his voice took him by surprise, but he'd been holding back so long because he understood she was nursing a broken heart. Even tonight, knowing she'd had more than her share of wine, he should be putting a stop to this but he couldn't. She was setting his blood on fire.

"Yes, yes, yes! I want you!"

"Then you shall have me."

Sweeping Miranda into his arms, Vaughn headed for the winding staircase. He took them two at a time until he reached the upper floor that housed the master suite.

When they reached his bedroom, Miranda was too overcome with emotion to say much. She just wanted to feel.

Feel Vaughn. Touch Vaughn. Kiss Vaughn. And Lord, did he know how to kiss. Her legs were weak as he lowered her to the floor.

She stood there, helpless as he spun her around. With her back presented to him, he tugged at the zipper of her dress and it fell to the floor leaving her once again in her thong and strappy sandals. While she stepped out of the dress, she watched him tug at his belt and impatiently shrug off his clothes and toe off his shoes. He was just as eager as she was to be together. She was still trembling when he drew her toward the bed and covered her mouth with his. She tasted bourbon. She tasted Vaughn and she relished the flavor.

Tonight, she wasn't going to hold back. Her hands groped blindly for his shoulders so she could wrap her arms around his neck. What had started as strong physical attraction had grown into something unexpected. Something she hadn't been looking for, but most definitely wanted.

Wanted Vaughn.

She heard a low moan which sounded like his, but she couldn't be sure. Could be hers. His kisses were beyond consuming; they were hot and passionate, and as their tongues tangoed, Miranda couldn't deny that desire was racing through her like wildfire and she could no longer deny that only Vaughn could put it out. He plundered her mouth like a soldier in the desert who'd gone without water but had finally found an oasis. *Her.* His hands weaved through her hair, bringing their bodies closer so she could feel the solid beat of his arousal and the promise of what was to come.

Waves of lust washed over Miranda as the kiss between them went nuclear. They ate at each other; all the while his hands moved down over her back, sides and back up again to hungrily roam over her breasts. She needed him desperately, wanted him in the most basic way a man and woman could be together. Her body was his willing instrument and she gave herself up to the skillful caress of his hands as they cupped the soft mounds. And when his tongue tantalizingly covered her taut aching nipples yet again and swept across them with wet lashes, Miranda didn't swallow her moan of lust. Pleasure of the purest kind escaped her lips when he rolled the engorged buds in between his teeth and tongue.

"Vaughn…"

Hadn't she always known it could feel like this—in her hotel room and again on their wedding night when Vaughn had begun making love to her? She'd known her body would melt for him if given the chance. And it did. His fingertips traced a path down the sides of her body until it reached the soft, tender flesh of her thighs. Willingly she parted them for him and when his hands found the place she was the most slick with need, a low murmur of satisfaction escaped her lips. She was so wanton with desire that she couldn't hide behind fear or shyness anymore. Instead, she abandoned herself to Vaughn and his hands. They explored her slowly and deeply, gliding and stroking within her slick walls. Miranda was lost in a maelstrom of sensations, especially when he fingered her while simultaneously sucking on her breasts.

Tiny quivers began to erupt inside her as his fingers went deeper, thrusting into her with deliberate intent. Demanding more and more of her. Miranda attempted to stifle her moans, but they were becoming louder and louder.

"Let go, baby," Vaughn whispered as his finger picked up the pace of the sensual torture until eventually any vestige of control was wiped away and she cried out her release.

Miranda was still shuddering when he began raining hot kisses down her belly and his head lowered to the curls at the apex of her thighs. At the electric touch of his tongue on her tiny nub, she arched off the bed, crying out something unintelligible.

His hot tongue circled her slick core, toying with the tight nerve endings, rendering her speechless as she sank into a sea of sensation. And Vaughn was right there to lap her up, over and over again until eventually her pulse quickened and her body erupted and spasm after spasm overtook her.

Chapter 10

Vaughn's mouth returned to capture Miranda's, kissing her softly and gently. He'd enjoyed how she finally let go of her inhibitions and consequently he'd given her two orgasms. And he planned to give her more. Brushing the damp tendrils of her hair aside so he could frame her face, he asked, "Are you okay?" Her whole body was still vibrating with the sensual pulse of her multiple orgasms.

She nodded, unable to speak, and Vaughn couldn't resist an inward smile. He'd made her dissolve and he loved every second of tasting her sweet honey. His hands slid down her body with slow mastery, caressing the flat panes of her stomach and the curve of her hips. She was his wife. His woman. And he would do anything to please her, including delaying his own gratification to ensure she was thoroughly satisfied.

Vaughn drew her close to him. He'd been taking it slowly but now as the blood roared through his ears, the time had come to possess her. Make her his. He traced her lips with his tongue and she gave herself over and pressed her open lips to his. A shiver rippled through him and his entire body throbbed, eager to be inside her.

He lifted away from her. "You're so beautiful," he said, his lips leaving hers to nibble at her earlobe, "And I want you so much…"

She reached upward to trace the contours of his face, lightly touching his brows, sweeping across his eyes and then coming to his jaw and cleft chin. She was tempting him beyond measure. "I want you," she breathed. "Please... take me."

Vaughn couldn't wait to consummate their marriage. He spread her thighs wider so his fingers could work her nub to be sure was ready for him. She was still slick with moisture and he couldn't wait any longer. Grasping her hips, he moved between them, tilted her to just the right angle and then drove inside her in one smooth thrust. Miranda arched off the bed, crying out at his possession. He shifted slightly and her body yielded as if it knew him, accepted him. Slowly, he withdrew only to thrust back again and she caught him. Her hands clutched at his back as she held on to him and kissed his shoulders.

When he began moving inside her with powerful strokes, the first flickers of pleasure shot through him. Vaughn could feel himself going deeper and deeper into the very heart of her. Melding and merging into a pool of hot molten lava that would soon erupt.

But he didn't want it over yet.

He slowed the pace even though her body, her hips were seeking, imploring him to go faster. "Vaughn!" She cried out his name and her eyes flickered open. He didn't know if it was a moan or plea.

"Yes, baby?"

"I need..."

He lifted his head to gaze down at her. Her eyes were smoldering with desire. "What do you need?"

"More."

For one long moment, he stared down at her. Passion glazed her eyes. Passion for him alone. It made him feel exultant that Miranda was finally able to reveal her true feelings.

And so he gave her more, quickened the pace, thrusting in and out, slowly and rhythmically. He was possessing her supple body and giving her everything he had. His hands moved down her breasts to slip between them and stroke her clitoris.

"Yes, oh yes." She moaned, gyrating her hips.

He could hear the slapping of skin against skin as he feverishly drove himself home and buried himself deep inside her. And just as if a trigger was released, she whimpered, sobbing out his name as she went over the edge of the precipice. She wasn't alone.

Vaughn gave a triumphant shout as he followed her over the edge.

Ring... Ring...

Several hours later, Miranda came back to reality too slowly. The feeling of utter bliss and satiation coursing through her veins was being disrupted by the annoying sound of the telephone. She felt the mattress dip as Vaughn rose and moved from the bed.

"What?" She heard only his side of the conversation. "A break-in?"

At those words, Miranda sprang upward, clutching the sheet to her bosom. Did he just say break-in?

"When did this happen?" She watched Vaughn head toward his enormous walk-in closet. When he emerged he was wearing a track suit and sneakers. "I'll be there in fifteen." He abruptly ended the call.

"Is everything alright?"

Vaughn walked toward her and Miranda's heart soared. This man. Her husband was her lover now. They'd just shared the most intimate moment a man and woman and could. So why was she suddenly embarrassed?

When he reached her, he sat beside her on the bed. "There's been a break-in at Prescott George. They were unable to reach our president, Christopher Marland, so now I have to go."

Her heart lurched. "Is it safe for you to go in his stead?"

"Are you worried about me?" he inquired, stroking her cheek.

She frowned in consternation. "Yes, of course. I wouldn't want anything to happen to you."

"The police are still there because they need me to sign some paperwork, but I'll be back soon."

He didn't say another word on how he felt about what had just transpired between them. Instead he rushed out of the room, leaving Miranda to wonder if he was regretting spending the night with her. Although the break-in wasn't his fault, he could have given her a kiss goodbye.

Something.

Some acknowledgement of the incredible experience they'd just shared. So she didn't feel so insecure about what she'd allowed to happen between them. Had she not been good enough? Or perhaps she was too much in the bedroom? Did he think she was a nympho? She had been wanton with Vaughn, clutching at his shoulders. He probably had scratch marks on his back from her exuberance during their lovemaking. It had been a long time since she'd been with a man and Vaughn knew how to use his hands and mouth so much so that Miranda had lost control.

Had she made a mistake by allowing their relationship to get physical?

Vaughn didn't know why he'd rushed out of the bedroom as if someone was chasing him, but he had. Yes, he needed to get to Prescott George's offices, but he'd also needed some breathing room. Space to figure out his feelings and how suddenly everything between him and his wife had changed.

But he knew inexplicably that it had.

Once he made it downstairs, he grabbed his keys and was out of the door and walking to the garage. Flicking on the lights, he glanced at his Ferrari. He needed speed.

A good dose of adrenaline to right himself. Turning the ignition, Vaughn kicked the car into gear.

The intensity of their lovemaking had been so strong. It was as if they'd been one heart, one body. Vaughn had been intimate with other women, beautiful, confident women who knew their way around the bedroom, but none of them were Miranda. They didn't have her sweet disposition. They didn't make him laugh and feel content whenever he was with them.

As he sped down the highway, Vaughn couldn't recall ever feeling this happy before and it was all because of Miranda. She was solely opening his eyes and he was seeing there was more to life than work, surfing and the occasional casual fling. But despite how incredible the sex was between them, Miranda constantly reminded him that their relationship was short-term. To want more, to even think about it was asking for heartache, but it didn't stop Vaughn's mind from wandering in that direction.

What would it be like if they were married for real?

What if there was no deadline to the end of their marriage?

When he arrived at Prescott George's building, there were two police cruisers with flashing lights waiting outside. Turning off the engine, Vaughn stalked purposely toward them. The two male officers looked sternly at him as he approached. The taller and more slender of the two spoke first. "Vaughn Ellicott?"

He nodded. "Yes. That's me. What do you have, Officer?"

"I'm Officer Coyle. This is my partner, Reinhardt." He motioned to the stubbier and portly gentleman at his side. "Come see for yourself. You can tell us if anything has been stolen."

Vaughn walked through the front door to find out how bad the damage was. He could see that the lock had been tampered with. He'd already called a locksmith on the drive and they would be here soon to replace it. The security firm he hired was also en route to review the security footage. There were cameras at the front entrance and throughout the offices; perhaps it would tell them who'd broken in.

"We have security cameras," Vaughn said as he walked in. He walked deeper into the main room, looking into each individual office with the police following closely behind him. The place had been tossed about, but as he scanned the room, there were no obvious missing items.

"Anything missing?" Officer Coyle inquired.

He shook his head. "Not that I can see at first glance, but our president and other board members will need to assess the situation."

"If nothing is stolen, could have just been some kids involved in criminal mischief. We get that all the time. Young kids with nothing else to do except cause trouble."

"Or maybe they were looking for something specific?" Officer Reinhardt offered.

Vaughn frowned. "Prescott George's headquarters isn't well known. There would be no reason for them to target us. I'd like to check the security footage. The cameras should have caught the perpetrators right in the act."

He was wrong.

The camera feed on the computer in the reception desk showed nothing. The thieves had disabled the security cameras. He turned to the officers. "This was no random act. Whoever broke in knew what they were doing. How else could they have known that there were cameras and how to disable them?"

"So you think it was an inside job?" Officer Coyle frowned, glancing at his partner. "Is there anyone in your organization that has a beef or gripe?"

Vaughn could think of plenty. There were a number

of the older members who thought the organization was going down the wrong path with their new recruits but he couldn't think of a single one of them who would take it this far. "No, Officer, I don't think so."

Officer Coyle shrugged. "Alright, well, if you'll sign this—" He pulled out a tablet for Vaughn to sign. Then he handed him a business card. "This has all the details of the police report and it'll be ready in twenty-four hours for you to pull online and submit to your insurance carrier."

Just then, there was a knock on the door and Vaughn could see a gentleman with the logo of the locksmith company on his shirt. "Thank you, officers." He shook their hands.

"If you think of anything, feel free to give us a call," Officer Coyle said.

Vaughn nodded. "I'll do that."

After he took care of the lock and ensured Prescott George's offices were secure, Vaughn returned home. On the way, he'd left a message for Christopher to call him first thing in the morning so they could discuss the incident. He had a hard time believing that the old-timers would go to these lengths. It had to be someone else, but who? They'd have to put their heads together and figure out who in their organization could be behind the break-in.

The house was quiet when he got home. Miranda must have fallen back asleep. His groin tightened thinking about his beautiful wife. Vaughn climbed the stairs eager to see her. He stopped by her bedroom first, checking to see if she'd run scared and gone back to her comfort zone. He was happy to find it empty.

He climbed one more flight and found her lying in the middle of his bed. However, sometime during the night, she'd gone downstairs and put on one of those silk nighties. *Had he been hoping to find her naked and waiting for him?* If so, he'd miscalculated. Instead, she was sleeping peacefully. Her hair was spread out around her like a halo on the pillow. She'd never looked lovelier except on their wedding day when she'd walked toward him in a confection of white tulle. He'd been breathless then as he was breathless now.

Making love with Miranda had been better than he imagined. The responses she'd made when he'd kissed her, touched her and licked her had called out to every primitive male instinct in him to possess her and make her his. And it was messing with his head. With every other woman he'd dated, he'd been in control of their relationship, but not with Miranda. He wasn't in control when he was with her and he didn't like the feeling.

His entire life had always been about structure, discipline and never showing his emotions. It was what the Commander had taught him and how he'd been groomed in the military. Miranda disrupted his well-ordered structure and made him dream, made him *feel*. And it made him uneasy. Vaughn didn't know how to show his feelings except in action. He could *show* her how he felt, but put it into words? That's where he faltered. Plus, he wasn't altogether sure she wanted to hear them.

He pulled off his track suit, tossing it carelessly across a chair, and joined her in bed. She didn't wake when he reached for her and pulled her toward him. Instead, she snuggled even closer to him. Although he wanted her in his arms, it was going to mean very little sleep. Since her arrival in his life, everything was not in the box Vaughn usually compartmentalized his life in.

How was he going to navigate the waters of their married life now?

Miranda awoke to find herself nestled in Vaughn's arms, one thrown across her middle keeping her firmly in place while her rear was planted solidly against his groin. She shifted, trying to move away, but Vaughn merely pulled her into his embrace and that was when she began to feel his morning erection. A tingle began in the pit of her stomach.

"Relax," Vaughn whispered from behind her.

Her heart jolted and her pulse pounded. He was awake? Could he hear her rapid heartbeat?

"How long have you been awake?" She was afraid to turn around and face him. Afraid he'd see just how much he affected her.

"Not long. Couldn't sleep much." And before she could react, he'd shifted her until they were facing each other. He looked drawn and tired.

"Because of the break-in?" She, on the other hand, had slept soundly after he'd made love to her so thoroughly.

He nodded. "I've been racking my mind thinking who could have done something like this, and come up empty."

"What happened?"

"Not much actually. Some things were tossed about, but nothing seemed to have been stolen. The police thought it might have been kids involved in criminal mischief."

"But you don't think so?"

His expression was introspective and he was silent for several minutes. "No." He shook his head. "This was no robbery. Nothing was taken even though there were plenty of expensive electronics. Whoever broke in knew what they were doing because they disabled the security cameras."

Miranda frowned. "Do you think it could be a member of Prescott George?"

"I don't know, but I'm going to find out." Vaughn tossed back the covers and jumped out of bed. He was bare chested and wearing boxer briefs and she couldn't help but notice his chiseled abs, tight behind and impressive package. She'd *felt* him this morning, thought he might even try for another round, but he hadn't.

Did he still want her? Had last night been a mistake? Or a one-off?

"What are you going to do now?"

"I have to go back to Prescott George and help clean up," Vaughn said and went into the bathroom.

Seconds later, Miranda heard running water as he took a shower, without her. Vaughn was acting as if nothing had happened between them. That he hadn't made her cry out and orgasm several times. *Could he so easily forget the intimacies they'd shared?*

And if he did, what did that mean for their marriage?

Chapter 11

Miranda needed a diversion. She was filled with dread over Vaughn's blasé attitude about spending the night with her. But could she blame him? The more she thought about it, she had been the one who'd insisted on a marriage of convenience and yet she'd changed the rules last night. He was a man after all and he hadn't resisted her advances. She'd known he'd wanted her and she allowed herself to give in to that need. And he'd fulfilled her every desire.

Was that what scared him away?

Not knowing how he felt or what he was thinking was driving her crazy and putting her on edge. Making her wonder if there was a way out of this mess. Perhaps she'd been too hasty in her decision to marry Vaughn. Was there anything she could do to end their misery? She knew it was a long shot, but she called her legal counsel in Chicago to see if they had found a loophole in her grandfather's will. Unfortunately, they gave her the same spiel they'd given her over a month ago, which was that their research hadn't yielded any results. There was no way around her grandfather's wishes that she marry.

Miranda felt trapped and had to get out of the house because everywhere she looked, she saw Vaughn and it hurt. So she decided to meet Sasha for lunch. They hadn't seen each other since the wedding when Sasha had tried to talk her out of marrying Vaughn and "making the biggest mistake of her life." Despite the awkwardness between her and her husband after making love, Miranda didn't feel that way. Because of Vaughn's generosity, she was getting access to her inheritance. Without him, all her hopes and dreams might have gone along the wayside. So if anything, she was grateful to Vaughn.

She met up with Sasha at a restaurant not far from the beach. Because of Vaughn, she'd quickly become accustomed to the fresh ocean air and the breeze that came with it. Sasha had already arrived and was sitting outside at one of the café tables underneath an umbrella. She rose to greet Miranda. "Hey, love," Sasha said with a kiss and hug.

"Hey, girl." Miranda returned the embrace and sat down across from her.

"How are you?" Sasha asked, raising an eyebrow. "You've been awfully quiet the last couple of weeks since walking down the aisle. How is married life?"

"Going good, going good."

A waitress came over with menus and took their beverage orders. Miranda focused on reviewing the menu, but could feel Sasha's eyes on her.

"That answer was a little too pat if you ask me," Sasha responded. "So let's be real." She leaned forward across the café table into Miranda's personal space. "You married a man you'd only known for barely a week and have spent the last weeks primarily in his company. You know I want the details. What's he truly like?"

Miranda put the menu down and settled back in her seat. "He's pretty wonderful," she answered honestly. "He's kind and respectful, thoughtful even."

"Those are some amazing traits. Are you surprised?"

Miranda sighed. "I guess I kind of am. I didn't know what I was truly getting into. Other than he had an admirable background in the Navy, came from a solid family and was richer than sin."

"You forget incredibly handsome," Sasha added with a mischievous grin.

Oh she hadn't forgotten that, thought Miranda. It was the *first* thing she'd noticed about her husband when he'd come out of the ocean and she'd been treated to his shockingly beautiful body. Those broad shoulders. Those incredibly powerful thighs. He'd had quite an effect on her then and now. When he was within a few feet, she could feel every part of herself. Her breasts would constrict in her bra and there was an ache in the lower half of her body. She was so much more aware of her physicality when she was around him.

"Yes, my husband is attractive."

"And does he find you attractive?" Sasha pressed.

Miranda blushed. Completely giving herself away. "Yes, I believe he does."

"Something tells me you more than believe," Sasha said, zeroing in on her reluctance to say more. "Have you kissed? I mean other than the wedding?"

"We have."

Sasha sighed heavily. "Jeez! Why are you making me pull this out of you, Miranda? You asked me to lunch because you have something on your mind. So tell me what's going on. What's got you so on edge? Or should I ask who?"

"Alright," Miranda sighed. "I admit that my relationship with Vaughn has progressed."

"You've slept with him?"

Miranda nodded. "Last night. But we didn't just hop into bed. We took time to get to know each other and so far everything has been going well."

"So what went wrong?"

How was it that Sasha could read her so accurately? They hadn't seen each other often since they'd graduated from college. Yet, her friend had hit the nail on the head. Was she that obvious? *And if she were, why didn't Vaughn pick up on her anxiety last night and this morning?* Instead, he'd rushed to the office. She understood he had to address the break-in, but the least he could have done was acknowledge what had taken place between them.

"I don't know." Miranda finally answered Sasha's question. "Last night was incredible." Her face colored admitting it, but it was true. "Better than incredible. But then he got a phone call about a break-in at Prescott George."

"The Millionaire Moguls club?" Sasha asked, leaning back in her chair to regard Miranda. "That's surprising."

"As soon he got the call, he rushed off."

"Are you upset that he left? Perhaps he was the only person they could reach."

"I know that logically," Miranda responded. "He had to go because they couldn't reach the president. But once he got back, he didn't try to wake me up and talk about it. And this morning, he didn't mention what had transpired between us. Was I just another one of his bed bunnies?"

"I highly doubt that," Sasha said. "He married you. Not any of them."

Sasha had a point.

The waitress set down their sparkling waters. They quickly ordered so they could return to the conversation.

"I know you're perturbed because he didn't acknowledge that you'd become intimate, but it's reasonable that he'd be preoccupied with Prescott George. It's a prestigious organization and something like this just doesn't happen to them."

Miranda frowned. "You make me sound *unreasonable*!" She didn't think so. "I would have just liked to know how he felt. Or if he regretted our time together last night."

"No, not unreasonable, just maybe more emotional than Vaughn. You know men are not highly evolved like us, Miranda. They don't recognize how serious having sex is for us women."

"I suppose."

"I'm sure I'm right. But let me ask you something. Are you regretting spending the night with your husband?"

They hadn't just had sex, not in Miranda's mind. They'd made love. What they'd shared had been beautiful and mind-blowing. At least to her. Perhaps Vaughn felt differently, but she didn't know because he hadn't deigned to talk about it.

"Miranda?"

"I heard you. I don't regret it," she finally said. "Or I didn't, but over the last twelve hours I've begun to have my doubts. And his behavior thus far hasn't helped alleviate my fears."

"Don't overanalyze it too much."

"What?" Miranda stared back at her incredulously. "You always analyze everything, Sasha. That's why you're such a sought-after marketing consultant."

"Precisely," Sasha said, pointing to her. "That's business. This is personal. I can't believe *I'm* saying this, but don't be so hard on Vaughn. Give him a little slack. He was forced to leave and turn his back on you to take care of something very near and dear to his heart. You don't know for sure that he has any regrets. When he gets home later, talk to him about it. Clear the air."

Miranda continued her lunch with Sasha. Perhaps she was in her head too much and being too hard on Vaughn. They were going to be married for the foreseeable future and she couldn't possibly continue with this ambiguity between them. When she returned home later, she was going to find out exactly how he felt. One way or the other.

"So you've no idea either who could have done this?" Vaughn asked Christopher when they met up later that morning. Over several hours, they'd made a lot of headway in getting Prescott George's offices returned to their normal state of order. Couches and chairs were back upright.

Paintings that had been hanging skewed on the wall were perfectly positioned. Papers that had littered the floor last night had been swept up.

"No, I've no idea," Christopher replied as he paced his office. As an officer of the organization, Christopher had his own office. "We've never had something like this happen before. Did the police have any ideas who could have done this?"

Vaughn shook his head. "They thought it was just teenagers causing trouble, but here's the thing, Chris. Whoever ransacked this place knew what they were doing."

"Why do you say that?"

"Because they disabled the cameras."

"So there's no footage of the break-in?"

"Nope. So it had to be an inside job. Someone in the organization or with access to Prescott George. There's no other explanation."

Christopher shook his head. "Vaughn, that's a crazy notion."

"No, it isn't," Vaughn persisted. "And it's naive if you think otherwise. Why would anyone trespass and damage property without taking anything?"

Christopher seemed introspective as he took in Vaughn's words.

"Nothing was taken. Surely you must see the truth in what I'm saying. We have the best and most expensive computers and electronics in this office. And thieves choose to throw things around, damage artwork, but not steal anything?"

"I guess you're right. Everything is accounted for, but how do we go about finding out the culprits?"

"Secretly," Vaughn said. "We need to identify a list of suspects and quietly investigate them."

"Investigate our own members?" Christopher asked.

His brown eyes filled with bewilderment. "I can't believe it's come to this."

"Neither can I, but we have to find out who it is, especially with our benefit coming up and announcement as Chapter of the Year. What's it going to look like if we're embroiled in a PR scandal?"

"I agree with you. I'd like you to hire a private investigator."

Vaughn didn't mind Christopher giving him an order. Prescott George was important to him and he would have been doing it on his own if Christopher still had misgivings. "I think it's a smart move."

"But I'd like to keep the results of the investigation between you and me. We won't reveal this to other members until we can ferret out who the culprit is. I think in the interim, we continue to suggest that it was just a teenage prank. Agree?"

Vaughn nodded. He shook Christopher's hand. "We'll speak soon."

Once he was sure Prescott George was squared away, Vaughn returned home. He was eager to see Miranda and have her back in his arms. Now that he had time to think about it, he realized their first night together had been cut short by this break-in foolishness and his own fear. He wasn't sure if he could recapture the magic from last night, but he could certainly try.

"Miranda?" He called out to her, but the house was empty. Vaughn couldn't help but be disappointed. He shouldn't have expected her to be waiting home for him, but he'd hoped all the same. In the meantime, he would catch up on some work, but first there was a call he needed to return.

The Commander had called while he was cleaning up PG's offices and Vaughn hadn't been able to answer him.

He wasn't happy with his parents. Their failure in not attending his wedding irked him. Vaughn understood that he'd given them short notice and that they weren't exactly excited at the prospect of him marrying a stranger, but they could have come anyway. Supported his decision even if they hadn't agreed, just as Miranda's parents had done.

"Vaughn," the Commander answered on the second ring.

"I'm returning your call," Vaughn started. "Was there something you wanted?"

"Do I have to have a reason to call my own son?" he responded sharply.

Vaughn sighed. He hated when his father got on his soapbox and spoke down to him, making him feel like he was eight years old again. "No, of course not, but considering we haven't spoken in a couple of weeks, I don't know what we have to say."

"Remember who you're talking to, Vaughn Ellicott. I'm still your father."

"You could have fooled me," Vaughn responded. "Why weren't you at my wedding, where a father should be?"

The Commander scoffed. "You know how your mother and I felt about your hasty nuptials. We were not going to participate or give our blessing to that sham."

Vaughn swallowed as anger rose inside him. For a split second, his vision went black and he had to remember to be respectful. "My marriage is not a sham, Commander. And you would know that if you'd taken the time to get to know Miranda instead of having preconceived notions about our relationship."

"Relationship?" His father laughed. "You hardly know the woman. It couldn't be that serious if you couldn't be bothered to introduce her to your own family."

"There wasn't time." The instant the words were out of his mouth, Vaughn regretted them.

"What do you mean there wasn't time?" His father latched on to his comment. "Vaughn, did you get that girl in the family way?"

Vaughn rolled his eyes upward. "As I've told you before, Miranda is not pregnant. I just meant that we were caught up in the moment and wanted to get married as soon as possible."

"I don't know," his father said. "Something doesn't sound quite right to me, but perhaps you're right. I could hold passing judgment until I meet your wife. Will she be at the Prescott George retreat?"

"Yes."

"Good. Then your mother and I will look forward to meeting her then," the Commander said. "In the meantime, why don't you fill me in on the break-in at Prescott George?"

How had he found out about it? He and Christopher intended to keep it hush-hush.

Vaughn was happy when the call with his father ended. He didn't like being on the receiving end of one of the Commander's interrogations. He'd much rather focus on when his lovely wife was due home, but she didn't arrive until later that evening, much to his chagrin.

It was nearly dinnertime when Miranda poked her head in his office. "Hey."

Vaughn glanced up from his laptop and enjoyed the view in front of him. His beautiful wife. Her hair was down with just a slight bit pinned up. She had on a bit of mascara and lip gloss, but wore no other makeup. She was wearing an amber color sundress which suited her creamy taupe complexion. The fitted bodice and swaying skirt hit just above her knee and showed off her toned legs. For a moment he imagined those same legs when they'd been wrapped around his waist last night as he'd buried himself deep inside her. "Hello."

"Are you busy?" she asked from the doorway. He noticed she was shifting from foot to foot. How could she still be nervous with him after the intimacies they'd shared?

"For you, no," he said, closing his laptop. "Why don't we get a drink?" He rose to his feet and strolled toward her. He placed his hand at the small of her back and felt her jump at his touch. And Vaughn didn't like it. He'd hoped they found solid footing over the last couple of weeks, but now it appeared as though they were regressing if she still tensed at his touch.

He lowered his hand and they walked side by side downstairs until they were in the large open living room. Vaughn set about making their drinks. Hopefully, it would ease the awkward tension between them. He handed Miranda the martini he knew she liked while he opted for something stronger, a bourbon. His wife sat on one of the plush white circular leather sofas and he joined her there. He was quiet, trying to assess her mood, but he couldn't read her.

She was closed off.

Her body language was too; she was sitting as far away as humanly possible on the other side of the couch.

"About last night…" Miranda began.

His ears perked up. He loved nothing more than to talk about it. No, he'd actually like to repeat it. "What about it?"

She took a sip of her martini and then set it on the cocktail table. "I don't blame you for what happened. I understand that we had an agreement, for a marriage of convenience and—"

She stopped, clearly at a loss as to how to go on, and Vaughn stared at her incredulously. *What was she trying to say? Was she trying to get out of their marriage?*

He didn't realize he'd verbalized his thoughts aloud until Miranda stammered. "No, no, I—don't want to end our marriage. I just don't want you to feel obligated to sleep with me. I understand it was a one-time thing and I know I had a bit too much to drink last night and came on to you."

Vaughn laughed aloud. *Was she serious?*

"Wh-what's so funny?" She looked truly crushed that he was laughing at her.

"Baby." Vaughn put down his drink and scooted across the couch, removing the distance between them. He grasped both her hands, sitting unceremoniously in her lap. "There was nothing distasteful about our night together. In fact, I'd like nothing better than to pick up where we left off."

"You would?" Miranda's eyes grew large with bewilderment.

"Yes, of course." He grinned at her. "I thoroughly enjoyed making love to you, with you."

"Then—then why did you rush off yesterday and again this morning?" she stammered. "You—you made me feel…"

She turned her head away, but he grasped her chin, forcing her to look at him. Her eyes were misty with tears and Vaughn hated that he'd made her feel this way. He'd been so caught up with Prescott George and his own feelings that he'd hurt Miranda and he'd never want to do that. "Miranda, baby, I'm sorry for making you doubt the way I feel about you, making you doubt just how much I want you. *Still* want you."

"You do?"

He could strangle the bastards who made her doubt herself and just how beautiful and sexy she was. "Yes. You have no idea how I've longed to be with you. How hard it's been for me keeping my distance these last weeks because you wanted a marriage of convenience, but I'm nothing else if not a man of my word. I would have kept it as long as you required. But last night, though, you showed me, told me you wanted me just as bad. Is that still the case or do you just want a marriage on paper only? Because that's not what I want."

Miranda's heart was overjoyed as she looked into the dark stormy eyes of her husband and saw desire lurking in those depths. He did want her! She'd gotten it all wrong. She'd allowed her anxiety and her past to cloud her judgment where Vaughn was concerned. He was a man of honor, a man of integrity. She hadn't made the wrong choice when she'd decided to walk down the aisle to him. She could admit her true feeling. "Yes, I want you, Vaughn. I need you bad."

His lips descended on hers, her breasts crushed against the hard planes of his chest. Her eyes fluttered closed as he deepened the kiss, taking her mouth fully in a greedy, hungry kiss. He left no part of her mouth untouched as he reacquainted himself with every bit of it. His lips teased at the seam of her lips and she parted them willingly. Meanwhile his hands slid lower, brushing her thighs as he made his way to the edge of her dress.

Miranda wiggled impatiently. She wanted him to touch her *there*, where she was molten and hot for him. "Please, Vaughn."

"Please what?" he said when his fingers took their time traveling down her legs to tease the backs of her knees.

"You know what," she stated. She was embarrassed to ask him for what she wanted.

He laughed huskily and then his hands moved upward underneath her dress. They slipped past the confines of her panties and then she felt him slide a finger deep inside her. "Vaughn, oh God." She writhed her hips against his searching fingers, hungry for more.

"Yes, baby." He moved from her lips and lowered his head to her breasts, which were already protruding through the soft material of her dress. He suckled one breast through the fabric and she arched upward at the contact of having his mouth on her and finger inside her, but he wasn't content. With a quick snatch, her panties disintegrated and Vaughn added a second digit inside her to tease her core.

Each delicious stroke gave Miranda unimaginable pleasure as sensation after sensation flooded through her and her dress began riding higher and higher up her waist. But Miranda didn't want to be selfish. Last night Vaughn had been an unselfish lover with her and she would be the same. She reached for his belt buckle and made easy work of it even though he was driving her mad with his mouth and fingers. When she freed him from the restraints of his briefs, she began stroking the hard ridge of his erection. She heard his involuntary intake of breath at her actions.

"Not yet, minx," he moaned, shifting her away from him. By doing so, it gave his fingers greater access to thrust harder and faster inside her.

Miranda tried to hold out, but he had her splintering apart within seconds and she gasped out his name. "Vaughn!" She contracted around his fingers and her head fell backward onto the cushions. All she could do was watch Vaughn drop his trousers to his ankles, not fully removing them, and join her on the couch. His shaft jutted out to greet her and in response she spread her legs and opened her arms to receive him. He moved over her and guided himself into her hot, sticky entrance as she rained hot, urgent kisses on his shoulder. He thrust in and out of her, finding a rhythm quickly while simultaneously teasing her clitoris with his fingers.

"Oh yes," she moaned. She couldn't keep quiet as Vaughn filled every part of her. It felt so good and she matched his urgency with her own need by gyrating underneath him. She explored the hard lines of his back over his shirt as she met his every thrust. Currents of desire coursed through her when he suckled her breasts again through her dress. Miranda came apart as her orgasm struck. Vaughn came right after her and thrust in her one final time, his groan loud and primal. He fell atop her, but quickly eased onto his side on the couch and held her to him.

They were both quiet at the reality of what just happened between them. She was still fully clothed with her dress bunched up at her waist, while Vaughn's pants were around his ankles and he still wore his shirt. Miranda had never felt that needy before, as if she'd die if she didn't have him inside her.

Vaughn was smiling down at her. "I like you like this."

When she could catch her breath, she asked, "Like what?"

"Wild. Free. Uninhibited." He leaned forward to brush his lips across hers. "That's how I want you when you're in bed with me." Miranda swallowed hard. She wasn't used to such blatant talk about sex especially when he said, "Promise me, you won't close yourself off to me, Miranda. You'll tell me or show me that you enjoy everything we do together."

She couldn't speak. All she could do was merely nod her head. And then Vaughn lifted her into his arms as if she weighed nothing more than a paperweight and carried her to the master bedroom.

Chapter 12

Vaughn couldn't remember the last time he'd slept in late because he never did. Because of his military training, he was usually up at the crack of dawn, working out or on his laptop. But he'd never felt this warm and sated. Earlier that morning, they'd reached for each other in the darkness, right before dawn when they were both caught between waking and sleeping. Miranda's fingers had made slow circles over his belly until they'd reached the rigid column of his shaft. Then she'd stroked him from the bottom to the head until he'd swelled to life and entered her warm, trembling body. He closed his eyes, remembering the way her silky soft skin had felt and how hot and wet she'd been as he'd bucked inside her. They'd both reached the pinnacle within minutes.

Lazily, Vaughn stretched and reached for Miranda, but the bed was empty. Cold, in fact, and Vaughn lifted his head in concern. He hoped she wasn't getting cold feet in the harsh light of day. He'd told her he didn't want a marriage on paper; he wanted a real one. But Miranda was ultrasensitive and he hadn't realized when he'd been preoccupied with the break-in that she might take it to mean that he didn't want her. Nothing could have been further from the truth. She'd consumed his attention nearly from the moment they'd met. And now that he'd gotten to know her, it had only grown stronger. He very much wanted to have sex with her.

Vaughn pushed back the covers and slipped on a pair

of boxers. Then he went in search of his wife. He found Miranda in the kitchen wearing a robe that barely reached her thighs. What appeared to be the makings of an omelet were on the large polished quartz surface of the break-fast island. There was a carton of eggs, spinach, onions, mushrooms and sausage along with several slices of toast she was buttering.

"Good morning," he greeted her with a wide smile.

"Good morning. Did you sleep well?" she inquired with a devilish grin as she halved the toast and put them on the plate.

"You know I did," he said, grabbing a slice of toast and happily munching. "You wore me out this morning."

"Who reached for whom last time?"

Vaughn chuckled. They'd made love on more than one occasion through the wee hours of the morning. This last time with her backside against his groin, he'd awoken and cupped her breasts. One thumb had grazed across her nip-ple while the other hand tangled luxuriously in the soft fuzz of hair between her legs and began to rhythmically stroke her slick, wet flesh. "Yes, I guess you're right. But I can't help it." He finished off the last bite of toast and walked toward her, pulling her into his embrace. "I desire my wife." His libido was in overdrive and he couldn't fight the impulse to have her here, now, on the bar.

Miranda pushed away from him. "Don't you start again! I have a frittata cooking in the oven and it's nearly done. I won't have you ruining breakfast."

"Oh c'mon." Vaughn snatched her back to him. "There's always time for a quickie." He glanced mischievously at the bar. "I could put you up here." He lifted her off her feet and placed her on the breakfast bar. "Kiss you here," he said. He opened her robe, happy she was naked under-neath, and lowered his head to kiss the valley between her breasts. "Suck you here." He lowered his head to one round globe and closed his mouth around one chocolate nipple.

"Oh…" she moaned and Vaughn used her distraction to move between her parted legs, while his mouth continued suckling her breasts. Miranda clasped her hands to his head to keep him in place. Then he eased the silk of her robe aside and slid one long finger along the sensitive seam of her cleft. He teased it with a whisper touch and loved how she jumped.

She gasped when his fingers delved deeper and eased inside. "We—we can't, not here, what about the—"

"Forget the darn frittata," he growled because the deeper he went, sparks were shooting behind his eyelids, threatening to drive him to his knees.

Miranda was overcome. She was a mass of tangled nerve endings. Because that was what Vaughn did to her. He made her want him, need him, inside her. He tugged his boxers down, grasped her hips forward and in one fluid stroke filled her in all the places that ached for him. Then he pulled her face to his and his lips began to mesh with hers, insistent and coaxing. Purring her approval, she hooked her hands behind his neck and tipped her face for his hot kisses. It was impossible to think with the thick fog of pure unadulterated lust clogging her brain. Vaughn began to move inside her, quick and sure at times, then alternating between slow and sensual, drawing out the moment.

His mouth was scorching but tender as he slanted it over hers, spinning a silken web of arousal around her. Would she ever see clear of it? The answer was no. *Who knew how long this feeling would last?* They'd entered this marriage knowing it had a set time limit, yet last night, Vaughn had indicated he wanted more. Miranda was afraid to believe him, to fully invest in their relationship. She would just enjoy it until the time came when she may have to walk away from him. Somehow, some way she would do so with her pride intact and without feeling as desolate as she did in her other relationships.

Her eyes slammed shut. She didn't want to think about the end. Not now. She would focus on Vaughn, her husband, no matter how short-term. She hooked her leg around his waist, opening even more and rocking against him. Then her sighs began to come quicker. She could feel the mind-numbing ecstasy taking over and she was powerless to escape its clutches. Instead, she rode the wave and Vaughn did too, groaning out his release as ripple after ripple tore through them. Vaughn hauled her to him as both their hearts galloped and they came spiraling back down to earth.

Miranda rested her forehead against his damp one.

Had they really just made love at the breakfast bar in the kitchen, for God's sake? There were more than enough rooms in the estate for them to never tire of locations, but that was what Vaughn did to her. He wanted her wild, free and uninhibited. Well, he'd gotten his wish because she'd never been this way with any other man.

"Are you okay?" he whispered softly.

Miranda nodded, though she felt so languid, she didn't think she could sit up. He must have guessed it because he wrapped her in his arms and carried her upstairs to the master bedroom. He laid her on the bed, but didn't join her and started toward the door.

"Where are you going?" she inquired.

He grinned. "To get the frittata."

Miranda couldn't resist letting out a soft chuckle.

Vaughn and Miranda slipped into an easy routine the rest of the week. During the morning, Vaughn would go to the beach to surf before going into Elite. Some mornings Miranda would accompany him because she'd quickly become adept at paddleboarding and she would be surfing in no time. He'd said she was a fast learner. Other times, he went solo to conquer the mighty waves, but when he did, he missed Miranda.

They were building on the sizzling hot attraction, which now that it had been unleashed was spilling over into the daylight hours. Just thinking of sex made him think of hot, hungry, insatiable Miranda. The sex between them was explosive. His body was starting to crave hers and Vaughn was having a hard time focusing on work because all he could think about was how Miranda looked in his bed, the way she felt beneath him, the sounds she made when he was buried deep inside her. He couldn't seem to get enough of her even though they were making love sometimes two or three times a night. How complete he felt when they were together. It was disconcerting, that this beguiling woman had come into his life and flipped the script on him.

Being in the Navy for a decade, he'd become used to the transitory nature of his life. He never got close to anything or anyone because he was frequently traveling the globe. Even once he'd left the service, he'd always felt an itch to move and could never keep still. However, when he was with Miranda, he could sit in one place. She didn't feel the need to incessantly chatter. She could be quiet and be still *with him*.

Miranda both scared and intrigued him.

Vaughn knew he was playing with fire by getting so close to the flames, but he couldn't resist her. There was inherent sweetness and gentleness in her that he hadn't found before. With other women, they would surely be seeking to lay claim not just to his heart, but to his home, but not Miranda. She hadn't even had all her belongings shipped to the estate. She seemed content to wear what she'd brought with her to San Diego or buy a few new things. Even though she'd inherited millions, she wasn't spending it frivolously.

Instead, Miranda was plotting and planning her next move, finding the right location for her B and B and ensuring her business plan was solid. She wasn't jumping ahead without thinking first. She thought things out except when it came to finding a husband. When Vaughn thought about what could have happened to her if she'd fallen into the wrong hands... Thinking about it made Vaughn ill. He was just happy he'd gone to the beach that day. Miranda was his.

His woman.

There was no other way to think of her. She was his. And only his.

And he wanted to do something nice for her as well as woo a potential company that was interested in Elite products. And he knew just the thing. He'd have Chef Jean cater a huge pool party at his house. And since Miranda didn't live lavishly, he would have a stylist come to the house with a selection of designer resort wear for Miranda to choose from.

Miranda was tickled pink when he told her his plan over dinner that evening. They'd taken to sharing the cooking. Some days Vaughn cooked and Miranda cooked the rest of the time. He'd never thought he would ever become so domesticated, but he was. And he kind of loved it. But that was only because Miranda was in the picture. What happened when she wasn't?

Vaughn shook his head. He didn't want to think about it. He would be content with the here and now.

"A party sounds great," Miranda was saying, reminding him he'd missed part of the conversation. "Do you need my help with anything?"

"No, babe. I just want you to enjoy it. Kindra is going to take care of all the details."

A pout spread across her lips. A pout he intended to kiss off. "But I'd like to help. I am your wife, after all."

"Don't frown," he said. "You are my wife and there will be plenty of other occasions for you to entertain. This weekend, though, I'd like you to just sit back and enjoy being lady of the manor."

She laughed. "Oh, is that what I am now? Your kept woman?"

"Oh yes, baby," he said, roughly pulling her into his arms. "And you're all mine."

The rest of the week went by swiftly. Kindra pulled the entire party together in a few days' time. On Saturday, the day of the pool party, catering and party trucks had already begun arriving around 7:00 a.m., disturbing Vaughn from his favorite task of morning sex with his wife. The house was bustling with activity and he steered clear by working in his office much of the morning, but came out to greet Miranda's beauty squad.

When she saw the entourage and smiled at him, Vaughn felt his heart constrict. Geez, he was falling harder and harder for his wife with each passing day!

Miranda couldn't believe that Vaughn had gone through all the trouble of hiring a stylist for her for a *pool party*. But it wasn't just any old backyard party. Vaughn told her the who's-who in San Diego were coming, including a well-known athlete who'd just won an NBA Championship and his supermodel girlfriend, the senator and his wife whom they'd met at Chef Jean's dinner gathering and several other A-list celebrities from musicians to actors.

Miranda wasn't sure she'd fit in, but she supposed that was why Vaughn had hired the very best in the business to dress her. The stylist hadn't come alone. She watched the makeup artist and hairstylist set up a pop-up station in the sitting room of the guest suite complete with a multitude of styling combs, brushes, flat irons and hair curlers as well as a variety of makeup.

She was going to be the most fashion forward woman at the party and according to the stylist every woman would kill to have what she was wearing and mimic her hairstyle and makeup. And as she peered through the racks of bathing suits, cover-ups and leisure wear, she believed it.

She sat down in the director's chair while the makeup artist set about doing her face. It was quite an ordeal from the cleansing, to the moisturizing to the foundation application to the eyebrow arching and various other contouring, highlighting and bronzing steps. Miranda had no idea what she would look like because the makeup artist was blending shades of eye shadow and lipstick while she worked on her face. The hairstylist washed and conditioned her and then set Miranda's long dark hair with curlers which she teased and styled so effortlessly.

Miranda was itching to see herself. It was another full hour before she could finally rise from her seat, but they still wouldn't let her look. Instead she was led to the bedroom, where the stylist laid out a sexy swimsuit and a two-piece outfit of an open, embroidered poncho and chiffon flyaway pants that would serve as her cover-up and outfit for the day. There was another dress if she wanted to change into something later on. Along with these killer shoes. He'd thought of everything.

A half hour later, Miranda had donned the entire ensemble, shoes and the accessories and looked at herself in the full-length mirror. She hardly recognized herself. They'd transformed her into a stunning creature. "Omigod!" Her hand flew to her mouth as she stared at her own reflection.

Miranda couldn't wait to show her husband and went in search of Vaughn. She found him in the backyard, which had been transformed into an oasis of lavish luxury. He was by the pool with the DJ ensuring the sound system was ready to go live. She was several feet away from him, but the look on his face when he turned and saw her stopped Miranda dead in her tracks. The look of appreciation on his face as he thoroughly evaluated her left no doubt in Miranda's mind that he was pleased with the result.

He began walking quickly toward her. When he was a few feet away, he motioned for her to spin around so he could get the entire picture. He must have liked what he saw, because he growled his appreciation. "That stylist is worth every penny."

Vaughn hadn't seen Miranda this dolled up since their wedding day. And even then, the wedding dress had covered all her assets, but today, now, she looked like a sexy goddess. The open top she was wearing gave him just a hint of the bikini without showing too much and the light flowing pants clung to her hips and thighs. How was he supposed to focus on business when Miranda was walking around like that? The only thing he wanted to do was take her upstairs and make love to her.

"I'm glad you approve," Miranda said. "It's no small feat to look like this. I've been upstairs—" she pointed upwards "—for the better part of three hours. I've never been primed and polished so much my entire life and that includes our wedding day."

Vaughn grinned. "I wanted you to have a special day. There will be a number of high-profile guests and although I knew you could handle it, I thought you might like having your own beauty squad to make you to look and feel your best."

He liked it when her face creased into a sudden smile. "I feel that way, thanks to you."

He pulled her into his arms and lightly brushed his lips

across hers, careful not to damage her makeup. "Then let's have fun today."

And that's exactly what they did. Kindra had ensured that his backyard was transformed into a tropical paradise. She'd brought in palm trees, tiki idols and seashells to give it that island flair. Meanwhile beach balls, floating rafts and a volleyball court had been set up in the Olympic-sized pool so that guests could have fun or just lie back and enjoy the water. Each guest was given some island concoction in a coconut that the master bartender had prepared.

Miranda was by Vaughn's side from start to finish and was the ultimate hostess. Chatting with the guests as they arrived, making sure everyone had drinks or tasted the delicious appetizers Chef Jean was in the kitchen preparing. Miranda had everyone eating out of her hands. She had natural, youthful enthusiasm that not only added to her charm, but made her alluring and sweet.

Jordan commented on it when he caught Vaughn staring after his wife. "She's something, isn't she?"

"Yes, she is." There was no hesitation in his praise. "When did you get here?" Vaughn asked, shaking his hand while holding his beer in the other.

"A short while ago," Jordan responded. He looked around. "Nice party you've got here."

"Yeah, it's been going rather well."

"But your wife is definitely the star. There's a disarming quality about her that makes it easy to talk to her," Jordan replied. "I found her to be quite delightful at Chef Jean's party. If you don't mind my saying so."

"I don't mind at all," Vaughn said proudly. He liked that other men were just a bit envious of what he had. Because Jordan was right. It didn't matter who Miranda was conversing with. She singularly gave them all her attention and focus so that they thought they were the center of her universe. "And did you bring anyone special this afternoon?"

Jordan shook his head. "I'm flying solo, Vaughn. Just wanted to make an appearance and support you. I'll have to get back to my studio because I'm working on a new piece that's taking up all my time."

"Of course, when the muse speaks you must answer," Vaughn said. "We'll talk soon." He was ready to find Miranda anyway, but she was so busy that Vaughn hardly got a chance to spend time with her for much of the afternoon.

Eventually, he caught her in the kitchen talking to Chef Jean and ensuring more appetizers were coming out. "Chef Jean, great work as always," he congratulated the celebrity chef. It hadn't been an easy feat for Kindra to get him to agree on such short notice, but Vaughn had made it worth his while.

"Vaughn, it was absolutely my pleasure," the French chef stated, "Especially if it means I get to spend time with your lovely wife." He kissed Miranda on either cheek. "She is a breath of fresh air, no?"

Vaughn looked at Miranda. Her eyes were alive and bright and he answered honestly. "Yes, she is." He pulled her away from the kitchen and into the corridor.

"What are you doing in here? You're supposed to be out there." He pointed to the party.

"I know. I was just helping out." Miranda looked sheepish. "Kindra looked busy entertaining your business clients and I wanted to make sure there were no missteps."

She didn't get another word in edgewise because his mouth blotted out anything she'd been about to say. He captured her soft lips with his, smoothing her moan of shock. Her mouth opened and he tasted the sweetness that was uniquely Miranda, causing desire to slam into him. Locking his fingers in her hair, he plundered her mouth. He was desperate with need and he used his mouth with erotic purpose to bring Miranda to the same explosion of need coursing through his veins.

Miranda pulled her mouth from his. "Vaughn, no. We... have guests." She glanced in the direction of the kitchen where any number of people could have seen them making out.

"Miranda..."

"Don't you know I have no control when it comes to you?" She dragged herself out of his arms and stepped backward.

"I kind of like that."

"Well, don't like it too much," she countered, "at least not now. We have all night."

"Promise?"

"Yes."

"Promises, promises, Miranda," he whispered as he took her hand and led her back outside, "because I intend to make you fulfill each and every one of them."

From the doorway of the veranda, Miranda studied Vaughn as he made his rounds to each circle of guests. Whether he was in the pool playing volleyball or playing chess with the NBA star, Vaughn was at ease wherever he went. Miranda had thought she'd feel like she was on show for the day, but surprisingly she hadn't. Being hostess and Vaughn's wife had come naturally to her as if she was born to do it. And she'd enjoyed it as much as she'd enjoyed kissing her husband when he'd backed her up against the wall earlier.

If there hadn't been a crowd of people, Miranda was sure he would have done something about it, but they hadn't. And now as the party was winding down, Miranda couldn't help feeling anticipatory as they said goodbye to their guests. The evening hadn't been solely about Vaughn either. Miranda had garnered quite a bit of interest in her bed-and-breakfast due to several movers and shakers at the party.

It was nearly two hours later when Vaughn and Miranda closed the door to Kindra and the last of the party vendors. They both sagged against the large glass doors. Vaughn turned and looked at her sideways. "Today was good. We make a great team."

Miranda smiled broadly. "Yes, we do." Then her throat felt parched as the look in Vaughn's eyes changed from tired to predatory.

"Are you tired?" he inquired, rising to his full height and walking backward toward the kitchen.

She shook her head. "No."

"Care for a swim?" He raised an eyebrow.

"Sounds marvelous."

They padded quietly outside and Vaughn released her long enough to switch on the pool's floodlights, surrounding them in blue light. Miranda peered up. The moon was high in a clear dark sky and suddenly the thought of a swim with her husband sounded irresistible. They'd had a pool party, but she hadn't actually gone into the pool. Even though she had on one of the most expensive bikinis she'd ever owned.

They didn't speak. Instead, they began to undress. Miranda slowly pulled the open poncho over her head and then slid down the flowing pants to her ankles. When she glanced up, she caught Vaughn watching her closely.

"I'd wondered what you looked like underneath that outfit," he rasped. "Now I know." He pulled down the pants he'd been wearing and dove into the pool. He emerged several yards away, his muscular torso glimmering in the moonlight.

Miranda laughed at his exuberance and walked to the entrance of the pool and padded down the steps toward him. She didn't care about her hair or makeup now. She only wanted to be with this man, her husband.

When she was inches away, he growled, "Come here!" And hauled her against him.

"Vaughn." Her skin prickled with excitement and not from the temperature of the water because the pool was heated. It was from being near Vaughn. She could feel her nipples turn to hard points even though they were crushed against his chest.

"Miranda…" he murmured. His eyes were intense and brilliant and her stomach flip-flopped. Those were the last words she heard because her eyelids fluttered closed when his hungry mouth pressed against her lips. He seduced her mouth with slow, practiced kisses because he knew exactly what buttons to push to get a reaction from her. She responded eagerly as she always did because the attraction between them was like nothing she'd ever felt before.

She didn't protest when Vaughn flicked his thumb over the hardened nub of her breasts. Instead, she moaned at how incredibly good it felt. And when he reached behind her to untie the top from her neck, she was glad to be free from encumbrances so he could have unfettered access to her breasts. She watched the top float away as he cupped her breasts in his palms, massaging and kneading them.

She wanted more, needed more…because desire was building, rising, swelling within her. Miranda never knew she could have this kind of binding connection to a man. That she could be so eager and open, but she was with Vaughn. When he lowered his head to lick, flick and tease her areola with his tongue, she threw her head back in abandon and moaned.

Then his mouth was back covering hers, deepening the kiss while his hands slid down farther over her backside and hips. Suddenly he carried her, weightless in the water, over to the steps of the pool. He laid her down while he set about removing her bikini bottom. She helped him by shimmying out of the wet fabric and he tossed it away.

Miranda was impatient for him to join her. She wanted him inside her. Now.

But he wasn't removing his swim trunks as she thought; instead, he was lifting her legs upward to rest on his shoulders, spreading them wide and then dipping his head between her aching thighs. She arched off the steps at the first touch of his hot tongue at her aching core. But he didn't stop there; he added his clever fingers to toy with her pulsing center and soon the world became a blur as Vaughn brought her rapidly to orgasm. Miranda cried out his name.

"You liked that?" he murmured when he lifted his head.

Her shallow breathing had begun to slow and return to normal. "Yes, but I need more."

He grinned. "Oh you do?"

"Yes, I need you inside me *now*." Miranda reached for the waistband of his trunks. She pulled them down in one swift motion and Vaughn stepped out of them. Her eyes grew wide at the hard heat between his legs, but that didn't stop her hands from closing over his velvety shaft. Instead of immediately taking him inside her, Miranda stroked him over and over again, watching Vaughn's eyes glaze over.

"For God's sake, woman, you're driving me crazy." He pushed aside her hand, lifted both her legs over his shoulders and thrust into her.

She gasped when he entered her. Vaughn thought he might lose himself as he filled her hot, tight heat. How was it possible that it got better every time between them? Every day, he could feel the control he'd always kept with other women slipping further and further away out of his grasp. Miranda had got to him. Because what had started out as a fiery physical attraction was morphing into something Vaughn hadn't been expecting.

Her sweet cries of pleasure filled the night air as he

moved over her, in her, bringing them both to the brink, before slowing down the pace. Miranda's eyes had drifted closed and she was writhing beneath him as the water lapped around them. Vaughn leaned forward and caught one of her taut nipples between his teeth and heard her sharp cry.

"Oh yes."

She was tightening around him like a vise and Vaughn wasn't sure he could hold out for a second longer, especially when she began to tremble and convulse. His entire body lurched over hers and his orgasm arrowed right through him as if he'd been shot with a bow. Vaughn had no choice but to cry out his release.

Slowly he disengaged from her and lifted her up into his arms. His intent was take her back to their room, but she coiled her arms around him and began kissing his neck. Grasping a towel, he led her to one of the nearby chaises and placed her on it. He couldn't believe he was already getting hard again. He bent to fasten his mouth on one cold nipple, before tantalizing the other with his teeth and tongue. When he pushed his finger inside her, he found much honeyed warmth surrounding him.

She was already ready for him and he didn't hesitate to ease inside her. She snaked her arms around him, bringing his mouth down to hers. Vaughn enjoyed kissing Miranda and lifted his head long enough to look down at her; the rapturous look on her face made him thrust in and out of her in rapid succession. Soon her body was contracting around his and he was jerking like a puppet as he emptied himself inside her.

Chapter 13

Miranda was falling in love. She hadn't known when she came to San Diego that everything she'd been looking for her entire life, she'd find in Vaughn. Since she'd been with him the possibilities had seemed endless. She was finding a sense of joy and accomplishment in her marriage. Vaughn had brought her into his world, opening her up not only to new experiences like paddleboarding and surfing but to new desires, as well. These tender new feelings were growing stronger each day. So much so that their lovemaking was not only physically gratifying but more exquisite than she could have ever dreamed possible.

Her belly knotted when she thought about how he could bring her to peak so easily. She recalled their passionate lovemaking after the pool party. Even though they hadn't been together for the better part of the day, she'd been edgy, needy. Watching him throughout the day. His face. His body. His mind. Although he had a body made for sin, he also had a brilliant mind. He'd carefully crafted who he'd wanted at that party and she'd seen him cultivating the powerful men over to his corner. It had been intoxicating.

So much so by the time he'd suggested the evening swim, Miranda felt as if she was intoxicated, and not by liquor, but by Vaughn. She couldn't wait to be alone with him because the kind of passion they had was all-encompassing, possessing her and making her its slave. Nothing in her life had ever felt as good as when she was in Vaughn's arms. Needless to say, she'd given him her all in the pool, on the chaise and again in their bedroom until they'd both passed out sweaty and spent with exhaustion.

But despite knowing how she felt about Vaughn, she had no idea of his feelings toward her. Was he in love with her? Because it was certainly how she felt. She knew that he desired her, wanted her. There was no denying that, but he hadn't revealed if his feelings toward her had changed. Not that she'd told him either. Out of pride or call it self-preservation, she was afraid to be forthcoming about her feelings. She was afraid of getting hurt.

It did beg the question: where did they go from here? They could continue as they were, content with companionship and amazing sex, but deep down Miranda wanted love and commitment. Family. Yes, family. Maybe not at this exact moment, she did want children someday. But did Vaughn? From the outset, they'd discussed what the marriage meant for Vaughn, the stability it provided to his business and his immediate family, but did that mean he wanted his *own* someday?

Miranda was afraid to bring up such a serious topic. What if he wasn't there yet? They hadn't known each other that long. They'd only been together a few weeks and in that time she'd finally turned thirty and according to terms of her grandfather's will, she'd received her inheritance. She was a millionaire and Vaughn had been there every step of the way cheering her on, supporting her. It seemed like she had known Vaughn her entire life. He was just the kind of upstanding, honest, loyal, dependable man her grandfather was hoping she'd find. It didn't hurt that he also happened to be sexy and handsome.

She was torn as to what to do. She would just have to continue with the status quo until Vaughn gave her a sign that he was ready for more. Miranda just hoped that they didn't run out of time.

* * *

"Any news about the break-in?" Vaughn asked the private investigator later that afternoon. He'd just attended a Prescott George meeting. All the members had been in an uproar over the incident. Once it had leaked to his father and the elder members, it hadn't taken long for the news to spread.

Christopher had alleviated their fears and assured them that the organization's information was secure and no personal information had been leaked. His reassurance that it was an isolated incident and was most likely teenage pranksters calmed the waters and they'd been able to continue on with business, which included discussing their next Prescott George outing this weekend at the winery.

Vaughn, however, still was uneasy which was why he contacted his investigator to get an update.

"I have a promising lead," the investigator replied. "The police found some traces of a chemical which is being analyzed by a third party lab."

"A chemical?" Vaughn was puzzled. They didn't have any chemicals onsite other than under-the-counter cleaning agents.

"At this point, we can't rule out any options," the investigator responded. "Because unfortunately, no other cameras in the area captured the break-in, so we're back to square one."

"There has to be something," Vaughn replied. "Whoever broke into the Prescott George offices knew their way around. How else would they have known how to disable such a sophisticated camera system?"

"I agree, but your members are some of the most affluent in the community," he responded. "There's no reason for any of them to vandalize property, but per your request I am checking into every member's financials to see if anything jumps out as suspicious."

Vaughn sighed. "Alright, I appreciate all your hard work."

Once he hung up, Vaughn was still uneasy. He couldn't put his finger on it, but he was certain that someone, a member of Prescott George or someone associated with them, was behind it. And if they were, what would prevent them from trying again? Maybe this was just a first strike. And maybe next time, the damage would be much greater.

He was happy when the day ended and he could go home to Miranda. As the weeks went by, he was more and more eager to see her when he ended his day. He hadn't known he'd been missing companionship until he saw her smiling face greet him when he walked in the door of their home. Today was even better, because she was wearing a tank top, skimpy shorts and an apron and greeted him at the door with his favorite drink. He hauled her to him and kissed her full on the mouth before releasing her.

"Thanks, babe." He patted her on the behind and tossed his keys in a bowl near the front door and followed her into the kitchen. The aroma coming from the stove smelled delicious. He couldn't resist sneaking over to the oven and having a peek.

"And how was your day, Mr. Ellicott?"

"Good. Had a meeting at Prescott George."

"How'd that go? Did you discover any more clues on the break-in?"

"No." He shook his head. "But we did talk about a Prescott George outing we have coming up this weekend. We'll be visiting local Baja wineries in the area."

"Oh yeah?"

"I would love it if my lovely wife could accompany me."

"I think that could be arranged." He heard the smile in her voice as she turned around to stir the contents in the pot on the stove. "If you're really good."

He liked the playful tone in her voice. "If I'm very good, what will I get in return?"

"You'll have to wait until tonight to find out."

He chuckled as he loosened his tie and then he dropped the bombshell. "My parents will be there."

"Oh." She didn't turn back to face him, but the tone of her voice had changed and was replaced with apprehension.

"They're looking forward to meeting you."

"Ya think?" she inquired with a raised brow, spinning around. "They haven't exactly put out the welcome mat. Though your sisters have all been very kind. They call or text just to check in on me, on us."

"Do they? I hadn't realized."

Miranda shrugged. "There was no reason to tell you until now. And don't get me wrong, I do want to meet your parents, but I'd be lying if I said I wasn't a little uneasy at the prospect. You've always made them or at least the Commander sound so daunting."

Vaughn paused. He supposed he had. "I'm sorry if I scared you. It's just that my father is not a man of emotion. He believes in structure and discipline. In duty to one's family, to one's country. And I suppose growing up in his household I've developed some of those traits."

"Not all of them," Miranda said softly.

"I've learned not to expect him to be warm and comforting," Vaughn said. "He's always pushed me to succeed, to be the best. In life, there's a winner and a loser, he'd say. So you must be the best. There wasn't any crying if you got a bad grade or lost a game. There was only 'do better next time.'"

"Sounds harsh."

Vaughn shrugged. "It's all I've ever known."

"And your mother?"

"She's always stood by my father. Though I will say

he was a lot lighter on my sisters, but being the oldest and a boy, the Commander was always a lot harder on me."

"Must have been a heavy load to carry, to always have to be the best, to never fail."

"That's why I didn't fail," Vaughn said. "Success was the only option."

Miranda nodded. "And love—did that ever enter the equation?"

Vaughn's heart started. The four-letter word he never heard in the Ellicott household. He'd only said the words to his parents when he was younger and they'd never returned them. And he couldn't remember the last time he'd had the courage to utter them let alone say those words to anyone. Sure he loved his family and he showed them how much in his actions toward them. That was his love language.

His silence must have been telling but that didn't stop Miranda from continuing her line of questioning. "Did your parents ever tell you they loved you?"

He frowned. "Why would they have to? They're my parents. They fed and clothed me. Put a roof over my head."

"I think parents should tell their kids they love them," Miranda offered. "Affirmations of love are very important to a child's, a person's well-being."

The topic of this conversation was making Vaughn uncomfortable and it increased when Miranda asked, "Have you ever been in love?"

"No, never," Vaughn answered almost immediately, maybe too fast for Miranda's liking.

"Never?"

He nodded to confirm as that was the extent he willing to go on this subject. He didn't know how their conversation had suddenly careened to family and love, but Vaughn was uneasy and he rose from the bar. "I'm going upstairs to take a shower." He started toward the doorway, but then paused to turn back. "Would you care to join me?"

"No, no." She shook her head. "You go right on ahead. I'm going to finish dinner."

"Sure thing. I'll be down shortly." Vaughn nearly trotted up the stairs to get away from the awkward conversation. He knew he was being rude, but he didn't know what was going through Miranda's mind. Something had set her off. And he didn't like it.

Why did she have to bring love into the mix?

Weren't they happy as they were?

Why did she have to complicate their marriage by bringing in the L-O-V-E word?

Miranda sighed heavily as she watched Vaughn go upstairs. She didn't know what had come over her, but she'd been like a dog with a bone pushing Vaughn for answers about his family. And it wasn't just about meeting the Ellicotts, though Miranda was nervous at the prospect; it was about a lot more than that. From what she'd heard over the last month and even tonight, no one had ever told Vaughn they loved him. And from the looks of it, he'd never said the words either.

So what did that mean for their marriage?

Miranda was in love with him, but hearing Vaughn speak tonight, she wasn't sure if he was capable of loving her in return. Sure, he could show her in and out of bed. That was the easy part, but to be open and honest with her about his feelings, to lay his heart bare? She wasn't sure Vaughn even knew how.

Was she banging her head against a wall and hoping for a different result other than a bloodied and bruised head. Or in her case, a broken heart? Had she once again fallen for a man incapable of loving her? He might not ever let himself love her and that would inevitably bring her the same pain she'd encountered in the past.

Miranda was quiet throughout much of dinner. Vaughn

had come downstairs damp from his shower and usually that would have been enough for them to have some hanky-panky before supper, but in this instance, Miranda wasn't in the mood. Her heart was heavy. Vaughn must have sensed her reluctance, because conversation between them was stilted for much of the meal. She was happy when it finally ended and she began washing up the dishes. It would give her an activity to keep her mind off what might not ever be.

She was deep into her own thoughts and finishing up the last pot when she felt a presence behind her. Vaughn wrapped his arms around her middle and bent his head to rain kisses along her neck and shoulder. He was trying to make it up to her the only way he knew.

And she let him.

Vaughn wanted her—he wanted her clothes off—so he could see all of her, touch her, sink into her soft body and lose himself inside her until she gave over to the desire between them. He'd felt her emotional withdrawal as they'd sat at the dinner table. It had never been that way between them. From the moment they'd met, they'd had a host of topics to talk about and never tired of each other, but tonight was different.

He could feel her pulling away from him and he wasn't going to have it. He cupped her breasts, abrading her nipples with his thumb over the tank top she wore. He was pleased when they puckered to life for him. "You were made for me," he whispered in her ear.

She may be angry with him over his responses to her questions, but her body could no more hide her attraction to him than any other time they'd been together.

She was his.

He tugged her closer so she could feel his imposing hardness against her tight tush. Then his hands moved to the curve of her breasts, down to her ribs and flat belly. When he reached the waistband of her shorts, he reached inside and touched her. Her breath hitched and she parted her legs wider so his fingers could nuzzle into the apex of curly hair at her thighs.

She moaned softly when his fingers slid inside. He thrust deeply into her again and again. He bent his head to suck on the soft spot on her neck that he knew was her weakness. Miranda shifted and he could feel her tremors take over her body, but she was holding back. He could feel it.

"Give in to me," he urged, stroking her harder. His fingers continued their quest, slipping in and out of her wet haven. She leaned her head backward against his shoulder and her hands clutched the countertop.

Seconds later, her cry echoed around them and he gentled her through her climax. Depleted, she sank against him and Vaughn lifted her into his arms and carried her to bed. She was silent as he undressed her and then himself before climbing into bed. He made love to her slowly, reverently until eventually she drifted off to sleep.

But he couldn't sleep. Because deep down Vaughn knew that a line had been crossed tonight and another line had been formed between them and he wasn't sure they'd be able to navigate their way back to each other.

Chapter 14

"Are you excited?" Vaughn asked Miranda as they drove to Prescott George's offices for the Baja wine tour on Saturday morning. The tour company was picking them up via private coach and would take the entire organization on a tour of three wineries with lunch included.

"Yes, it sounds like fun," Miranda responded. She was doing her best to reengage with her husband. Since their love conversation several nights ago, there had been tension between them. Though it hadn't manifested itself in the bedroom. There they were completely in sync and Vaughn easily both excited and surprised Miranda with his creative lovemaking. It was afterward that they'd been struggling to get back to where they'd been before.

She knew she was putting too much pressure on their new, fragile marriage, but Miranda couldn't help but be disappointed by Vaughn's feelings on the subject of love. She certainly hadn't broached the subject again for fear any intimacy between them would be completely gone. But deep down, Miranda knew that she'd pulled back from their relationship. She had to, otherwise she'd fall deeper and deeper in love with her husband.

They arrived to the brewery fifteen minutes later to a large gathering of Prescott George members, wives and significant others. Vaughn introduced Miranda to members who hadn't attended their wedding or the pool party. Miranda was thrilled when she saw Jordan, a familiar face in the crowd, with yet a different woman on his arm for the day. But it was Vaughn's parents she was most nervous to meet.

She knew his father instantly because he was taller than the rest of the men. He was shorter than Vaughn by a couple of inches, but had his same warm brown coloring and broad shoulders, yet not his physique because he had a few extra pounds around the middle. The Commander was dressed casually in khaki pants and a polo shirt. He was walking toward them with Vaughn's mother, a petite woman who was taller than Miranda by several inches. Her hair was in a sophisticated bob and reached her chin and she wore a matching rose-colored short set.

Miranda felt Vaughn tense as his parents came near. "Commander." Vaughn shook his father's hand and gave his mother a kiss on the cheek. "Mom."

Did he not call him Dad?

Vaughn turned to Miranda at his side. "I'd like you both to meet my wife, Miranda."

Miranda came forward to greet them. "It's a pleasure to finally meet you both." She leaned forward to give his mother a hug, which was responded to with a quick pat on her back while Vaughn's father offered her his hand.

"Nice to finally meet you, young lady," his father replied, shaking her hand. "I've been curious to meet the woman who could convince Vaughn to marry her after knowing him such a short time. You must be quite a woman indeed." He eyed her up and down. Not in a lecherous fashion, but Miranda certainly didn't get the warm fuzzies.

She smiled halfheartedly.

"Well, we should all get to the coach." His mother motioned them toward their mode of transportation for the day. "It looks like they're starting to load."

Vaughn grasped her hand and led Miranda to the coach bus. She was thankful for the contact because she couldn't tell what sort of first impression she'd made on his parents. They were certainly a cold pair. No wonder Vaughn didn't know how to express love and affection because he'd never received it.

Once they were on the bus, the jovial members and spouses laughed, talked, even sang songs on the less than two-hour ride to the Valle de Guadalupe. The view was spectacular. Miranda loved the rugged mountainside terrain along scenic Highway 1. But she especially liked that there was a mix of age groups from members in their fifties and sixties to Generation Xers and millennials. Miranda liked the diversity and commented on it to Vaughn.

"It's not always easy dealing with such a broad spectrum of viewpoints," he said in her ear over the hum of the engine and conversations.

"I'm sure it's not, but it's good to see you come together in a united front."

"I'm glad you're here with me." He leaned over and brushed his lips across hers in the sweetest of kisses. Miranda's heart fluttered in her chest. It wasn't a kiss meant to entice; it was a kiss meant to soothe. And it did; she looked up at him and smiled.

The day turned out to be wonderful. The first two wineries they visited were spectacular, with rolling hills and acres and acres of grapes that were grown and harvested. They started with a brief audio-visual presentation, then had a guided walking tour of the facility so they could see the wine-making process and how the wine was bottled and labeled. Then the tour guide showed them the catwalk so they could view the production areas, followed by a wine tasting of the region's premium wines.

Vaughn stayed by Miranda's side and they tasted the different selections together, commenting on which ones they liked or didn't like. They even explored the wine caves together, sneaking in kisses when no one was looking. It was the most relaxed they'd been over the last few days.

Eventually they stopped for lunch at an authentic Mexican restaurant. Miranda suspected they were going to have to sit with Vaughn's parents so they could get to know her, and she was right. The waitress sat them at a four-seater table and brought over a pitcher of sangria and poured them each a glass.

Miranda was thankful for some libation to get through the lunch. Throughout the day, she'd tried to make polite conversation with them, but had received a chilly reception. Maybe lunch would be different.

"So Vaughn tells us your family is well-respected in the Chicago community," Commander Ellicott began.

Oh Lord, it was going to be the Spanish inquisition, Miranda thought.

"Yes, the Jensens have been part of the Chicago framework for decades. My great-grandfather Thomas Jensen started the company many years ago, but it's run by my father now."

"Very impressive," Mrs. Ellicott responded. "And what is it you do, dear?"

"I have my MBA from Brown University and I work as a hotel administrator in Chicago."

His father frowned and his tone was curt when he asked, "Why not work at your family business?"

"Commander…" Vaughn spoke, but Miranda patted his hand.

"I don't mind answering," she said. "I wanted something of my own that I could take pride in building. I have my own hopes and dreams, Commander Ellicott."

"That's all fine and good, but being loyal and committed to one's *family* is the hallmark of upstanding character."

Miranda sucked in a deep breath. *Was he calling her character into question because she'd chosen not to work at her family's company?* Miranda rose to her feet. "If you'll excuse me for a moment, I need to powder my nose." She hoped the Commander would appreciate the good manners her mama had instilled in her, because she'd much rather pour the pitcher of sangria over his father's head at his rudeness.

Vaughn and his father both rose as she exited the table.

Fury boiled in her veins at his audacity. His father knew nothing about her, but yet he was willing to pass judgment on her? Or maybe he was just determined not to like her since Vaughn had gone against his wishes and married her anyway? *How was she supposed to get through lunch with that kind of acrimony?*

Miranda spent an extraordinary amount of time in the bathroom, taking a deep breath, texting Sasha about Vaughn's parents and wishing lunch would miraculously be over in the blink of eye.

It wasn't.

Painfully, she got through the meal and the Commander's continued questions about her family, background, schooling and religion. All of his questions were so impertinent, but Miranda answered them anyway. Her hope was somehow his parents might grow to like her if they found her to be open and forthright. And she would do this—for Vaughn, because she loved him.

Vaughn was grateful when lunch ended. Poor Miranda had been subjected to a battery of questions by his father who was relentless in his quest to find out about his wife. In his mind, no woman could ever measure up or be good enough for Vaughn except maybe the one he picked.

Fat chance.

Vaughn lived by his own rules and his days of listening to the Commander were over.

His parents were now chatting with several of their

friends, leaving him and Miranda in peace to enjoy the third and final winery.

"Thank you, by the way," Vaughn said when it was just the two of them again.

"For what?"

"For putting up with my father," he responded. "I know he can be a bit much."

Miranda chuckled. "That's putting it mildly."

She turned away from him, but he grabbed her by the arm. "No, seriously, Miranda. You were a good sport today. Don't think it went unnoticed."

She smiled at him in what appeared to be the first genuine smile he'd seen over the last hour during lunch.

"So it looks like married life is going well for you, Ellicott," one of the members of the club said when he approached.

"Marriage is going swimmingly," Vaughn answered smoothly, "My wife and I couldn't be happier. We're going to have a long, happy life together." He bent down and kissed her.

Once the man had gone, Miranda pulled out of his embrace and stalked away from him. What happened? He'd thought he'd smoothed the waters from the nightmare of a lunch. Was she still smarting over his parents' cool reception toward her? Didn't she know that he couldn't care less what they thought? *He* wanted Miranda and she wasn't going anywhere. If he had his choice she'd stay with him forever.

Forever.

He'd never thought about long-term with his previous relationships. Before Miranda it was all about recreational sex and the diversion it brought him when he wasn't surfing or building Elite. There'd been no commitments. No promises. No emotions. He only met up with women when it was convenient. And when he was satisfied, he moved on. He could go weeks without needing to see or speak to a woman, but in a short time Miranda had him looking toward the future. A future that included her. Maybe even a few children.

Children.

Whoa! They wouldn't come for a long time. He wanted time with his wife alone before the rug rats came so he could have plenty of time—weeks, months, years—to satisfy this constant hunger he had for her.

Maybe he was getting ahead of himself.

Staying married to Miranda was life-altering. If they stayed married he could lose focus, lose his edge because recently he'd forgotten everything except the pursuit of pleasure that he found when he was with her, inside her.

Vaughn glanced at Miranda as she talked to Jordan and his newest girl. Even now, he wanted to take her up against one of those barrels, have her wrap her legs around him and drive inside her. He wanted to hear her cries through the wine cave.

He needed to get a grip. It was just sex. Good sex. Mind-blowing sex. So why did he feel like it was more? Could it be more if he was only willing to allow it?

Vaughn walked over to Miranda and Jordan and slid his arm around her waist. This time when she tried to move away, he didn't let her, keeping her solidly next to him. She glanced up at him with those big brown eyes and he almost forgot there were other people in the room.

"So what did you think of that Cab?" Jordan asked with a smirk as if he knew something Vaughn didn't.

"Pardon?" Vaughn hadn't heard a word, he'd been so engrossed in trying to read Miranda's expression, figure out why she'd suddenly gone cold on him again.

"The Cabernet Sauvignon?" Jordan said, indicating the glass in Vaughn's hand.

Vaughn nodded in understanding. "Oh yes, it's good. Smooth."

Jordan smiled and glanced at Miranda. "We'll speak soon and if you really are interested in displaying some of my artwork in your B and B, let me know." Seconds later, he was gone.

"You're working with Jordan?" A stab of jealousy coursed through Vaughn. And he didn't like it. He didn't want any man sniffing around what was his. And that's what Miranda was. His. His woman. His wife.

Miranda smiled as she extricated herself from his embrace. "Possibly. I'm very interested in Jordan's work."

Vaughn's eyes narrowed. "What's going on, Miranda? Is my touch not what you would like today? Or would you care for someone else's?" His eyes trained on Jordan.

"That's ridiculous, Vaughn," she hissed when she saw the direction his eyes moved to. "And you darn well I know it. I haven't given you any reason to think I'm unfaithful."

"Except shrink away from my touch. And give me the cold shoulder for days."

Her eyes clouded, but then a sudden anger flared in them and her voice rose a fraction. "That's not true. And I would remind you that now is not the time to talk about this."

He glanced around and could see his father quietly regarding him from across the room. "Fine, but we'll talk about this later."

"Fine."

When they got back home tonight, Vaughn intended on getting to the root cause of Miranda's anger and mood shift over the last week.

Miranda silently seethed on the drive back from the Valle de Guadalupe. She refused to give Vaughn's parents the satisfaction of seeing discord between them so she played the part of dutiful wife and put a smile back on her face on the coach bus. But on the ride back to their home, tension filled the sports car. How could he for a second think she'd look at another man?

Couldn't he tell, couldn't he see how much she loved him?

She could never give herself to another man so completely without love; she supposed it was easy for men to have sex without strings, but not her. She was a different kind of woman. She needed love, respect and trust. She appreciated that they had a wonderful companionship. She just wanted more.

When the vehicle came to a stop, Miranda bolted and walked quickly to the front door. She was fumbling for her keys when he came around and said, "I got it." Seconds later, he was holding open the door for her to go through.

She didn't glance up at him and walked inside. She was about to walk up the stairs when he stopped her. "Miranda, I'd like to talk to you."

She paused on the staircase. Her hand trembled as it clutched the railing, but she slowly turned around to face him. "Do we have to, tonight? It's been a long day."

"Yes, we do."

Miranda sighed and began descending the stairs. She followed him as he made his way to the living room and sat down on one of the sofas. Miranda blushed thinking about just how many times they'd put the sofa to good use.

"You want to tell me what's going on?" Vaughn inquired.

"I don't know what you mean."

"Let's not play games, Miranda. You've been distant with me for days now and again during the wine tour, I could feel it."

"How can you say that?" she asked. "We've *been* together."

Vaughn's eyes narrowed. "Yes, I've had your body, Miranda. And we're good together in bed as I always knew we would be, but something is different. Something has changed. I can feel it and I know you have to, as well."

Miranda closed her eyes. He was right. And hiding from him wasn't doing them both any good. But she also didn't want to lose what they had either. She was in a precarious position. Yet she knew what she had to do, what she must do, no matter the cost. There was no way they could go on for the next eleven months this way, not after all they'd shared.

When she opened her eyes, tears were brimming at the surface. Vaughn instantly reached for hands. "Tell me, whatever it is, Miranda. For God's sake, just tell me what I've done wrong so I can make it better."

She shook her head. "You—you can't," she sniffed. Because you couldn't make someone love you back. She knew that. She'd tried miserably.

"Baby, please, talk to me."

"I don't want our marriage to be pretend," she started. "I want a real marriage."

"I want that too," Vaughn said. "And I thought that's what we've been doing."

"On the surface, yes, we have," Miranda said. "But I want more."

Vaughn frowned. "How much more? I've been sharing my life with you, my business, my passion, my organization. What more do you want from me?"

"I want your love," Miranda said softly.

Vaughn didn't immediately say anything; he just stared and looked at her like a deer caught in the headlights. For a moment, her heart dared to hope that he might feel the same way, might say that he loved her, needed her. Instead of just wanting her. She knew they shared a hot and explosive connection. She knew his body probably better than she knew her own. She knew what he wanted—be it her mouth, her tongue or her hands.

She knew when he wanted to make love softly and gently.

And she knew when he wanted to dominate and possess her.

When he remained silent, she continued. "I want to be more than just a body that you enjoy making love to."

"That's not fair." He finally spoke. "You've shared your hopes and dreams with me. You know darn well my attraction to you is not just about your body, though I do love your hips and breasts and thighs... Jeez." He sighed. "This isn't coming out right. You're one of the smartest women I know, Miranda. You have a brilliant mind and you're going to make an incredible businesswoman."

"But?"

"Why does there have to be a 'but'?"

"Because there is. I can feel it."

Vaughn rose from the sofa. "You're making this into a bigger argument than it has to be. Perhaps we should table this discussion until the morning. You're overtired and need some rest. It's been a long day."

"Don't try to placate me, Vaughn. Like I'm a child that needs a nap. I know what I want. I want a real marriage based on love, trust and respect. And the reason I want it is—is..."

"Is because of what?"

"Because I love you," Miranda answered honestly. "There. I said it out loud and the earth didn't tilt on its axis." The words had fallen from her lips with ease because they were heartfelt. "I love you, Vaughn. And the more time we've spent together the more that love has only grown stronger."

"Miranda."

"I know it comes as a shock because I'm the one that insisted on a marriage of convenience and I know that I kept harping on a year-long marriage between us. But the thing is, somewhere along the way, it changed for me and I began to want more. And I guess I'm just hoping that you might feel the same way."

She hazarded a glance in his direction and his expression was unguarded and held confusion. Miranda stood and walked over to Vaughn. She placed her hand on his cheek. The emotion she saw there was raw and was akin to something close to fear. Then he stepped away from her.

Love.

Now there was a word he hadn't expected to hear, least of all from Miranda, who'd always claimed their marriage was temporary. She was always the one reminding him that there was an expiration date to their union, while he, on the other hand, had been trying to get her to see that what they shared was rare and worth keeping.

But now that it was here in front of him, Vaughn wanted to run in the other direction.

He didn't know how to love. Sure, he loved his parents, his sisters and Prescott George. Hell, he'd even loved his country and had been willing to do anything to protect the United States of America, but romantic love? He was in foreign territory.

Lust he could understand. Like just now when her heavenly form had walked toward him, his eyes had fixed on the sway of her hips and the delicious rhythm they made. But more than that? He couldn't do it. "I'm sorry, Miranda, but I don't reciprocate those feelings."

A raw sound of anguish escaped her lips and Vaughn hated that he was the cause of it. Her hand flew to her mouth and he wanted to rush over to her and comfort her, but he couldn't. He had to be honest with her. "I'm not capable of that emotion. I'm just not wired that way. Never have been. And never will be."

Tears were streaming down her cheeks. "You don't know that."

"Yes, I do. And you've been around me long enough to see that. Look how I was raised!"

"No!" She shook her head, covering her ears with her hands, but Vaughn moved toward her and pulled them away.

"You must listen to me, Miranda. You must hear this. You saw my parents today. They've been married forty years and does it look like they love one another?" He sighed. "And maybe they do in their own way, but they've never shown it, to me or to my sisters. And so I've learned to live without it. I don't need love in my life."

"That sounds pretty cold and unfeeling." She sniffed.

"But honest," Vaughn stated. "I care for you deeply, Miranda, and I see a future with us doing great things, but you mustn't want any more than that, because I don't have it to give."

"You mean you won't give it."

"No, I meant I don't do the love thing and I don't know *when* or *if* I'll ever be ready for anything deeper. So you'll just have to accept me for who I am, flaws and all."

"Accept a marriage without love?"

"Yes, but that's not all that's on the table and you know it." He walked toward her, pulling her into his arms. He grasped her face in his palms. "What we've shared the last month has been incredible, the long talks, our fun times at the beach, the endless nights of making love…" He stroked her cheek. "Surely that is enough to build on and for us to have a happy life."

Miranda wrenched herself out of his arms. "It's not," she cried. "It's not enough and never will be. I would be giving up everything to be with you and you're not even willing to walk out on the ledge with me. Why are you running from your feelings, Vaughn? I know you must feel something more for me. I can't imagine that we'd be this close if you didn't."

"You're wrong. I'm not scared. I've never been scared a day in my life. For God's sake, things are fine the way they are, Miranda. Can't we just leave well enough alone? Because quite frankly I don't wish to change our arrangement."

"Well, I do." She pushed past him and ran up the stairs. Vaughn waited several beats and realized he couldn't let the night end like this. He had to talk to her, get her to see reason. So he took the stairs two at a time until he reached the master suite, but their bedroom was empty. The bed was still neatly made as it had been before they'd left for the wine tour.

"Darn it!" Vaughn kicked the post on the bed and a loud yelp escaped his lips. Miranda had returned to the guest room. She had returned to a room she hadn't occupied for weeks now. He wanted to go downstairs and haul her to him and make love to her until they couldn't see straight, but if he did, they would be still be in the same place they were now.

At an impasse.

Did this signal the end of their marriage?

Had he lost her for good because he wasn't capable of love?

Chapter 15

Miranda awoke the next morning feeling worse than when she'd found out her inheritance and fate rested with some unknown husband she'd yet to meet. But today was so much worse because it was like she'd gone to the mountaintop, had a taste of heaven before it was violently ripped out of her grasp. Because that was exactly how it felt last night when Vaughn had told her that he didn't love her and didn't know if he ever could. Just remembering it made her eyes sting.

How was their marriage going to last?

How was she?

She loved Vaughn, but it was all one-sided. They didn't want the same things. Love. Family. Children. He wanted sex and she'd suffice. A hot, warm body in his bed and who happened to have a brain. While she had fallen head over heels for him. But then again Vaughn was an easy to man to love. He was proud and strong and so confident. Some might think he was arrogant, but not Miranda. She found his zest for life refreshing. He was ambitious, always looking to succeed, to do better, and be better. It was intoxicating, charming and addictive.

So addictive. Miranda hadn't realized she was in love with him until it was too late. There was no way to protect her heart. She'd become vulnerable to Vaughn and the feelings he'd evoked her. He had only to touch her and her entire body would tighten in response. He had just that effect on her. And he knew it. She'd shared more with him than she had with any other lover, but she couldn't go back to being that pathetic woman waiting for scraps that the men in her life threw her way. She wouldn't beg and plead for things to be different. She had to be strong, show some pride just as Vaughn had taught her. She wouldn't accept a halfhearted marriage. It was too high a cost. Instead, she would do something about it.

Miranda reached for her cell phone and called her attorney.

"Miranda. I admit it's a surprise to hear from you."

"It shouldn't be," Miranda responded. "Nothing has changed. I still want to know if you've found a way out of this marriage."

"Kindra, these figures are all wrong," Vaughn said as she sat in front of him. "I told you I wanted to see next year's projections."

Kindra pursed her lips. "That's what I gave you, Vaughn."

"Well, these can't be right. They are showing a loss."

"With the spring suit line being new and all, the sales department is reluctant to project a large growth in the first year."

"I don't care what they think. I asked for them to include a five-percent spike in sales and that's what I want to see." Vaughn handed her back the folder. "Correct it."

"Of course." Kindra rose to leave, but Vaughn stopped her.

"And where is Elite's monthly financial report?"

Kindra leaned over and sorted through the myriad files on his desk and handed it to Vaughn. "It's right here. Is there anything else?"

Vaughn rolled his eyes. "No, that'll be all."

Several moments later, Kindra was gone and Vaughn slumped back in his chair. He wasn't angry with Kindra. She was the best assistant he could ever ask for. He was mad with himself. He was mad that he'd slept alone last night in a king-size bed that had suited him just fine until a certain brunette came into his life. And now, she had him snippy with his workers and that wasn't the kind of boss he wanted to be.

Vaughn jumped up from the chair and began pacing the room.

Miranda hadn't slept beside him and had chosen to stay in the guest bedroom instead. Vaughn didn't know for how long, but he didn't like it. And he doubted she did either. He knew she liked curling up beside him as he wrapped his arm around her middle. It was her favorite position.

His too.

And he wasn't going to let her throw away what they had. Up until this point, women had been abundant and interchangeable, in his opinion. Or at least they used to be before Miranda. But circumstances had changed. He didn't know when but he knew that Miranda was a big part of his life and he wanted her to stay. In their bed and in their marriage. She would have to accept that there were limitations, but that he would always be faithful and loyal. If she could accept that, they'd have a wonderful life together. So how did he convince her of that?

He was thinking about what he was going to do when the desk phone rang. "Ellicott," he answered.

"Mr. Ellicott?" The voice on the end of the line sounded perplexed. "Oh I'm sorry. I must have dialed the wrong number."

"Who is this?"

"This is Carl Alexander."

Vaughn's ears perked. He was the attorney from the law firm that represented Miranda during their premarital negotiations. He'd been surprised when Vaughn indicated he wanted no part of Miranda's inheritance and was willing to sign over any claim to it. "Mr. Alexander. Why are you calling?"

"I didn't mean to contact you. I was calling your attorney and must have inadvertently dialed you."

"And why would you be calling my attorney?"

"To go over some paperwork matters. Please forgive me." He attempted to hang up, but Vaughn didn't let him.

"All our paperwork was addressed before the marriage," Vaughn responded. "So has something new occurred?"

"No, but we found a loophole..."

When he hung up the phone several minutes later, Vaughn was livid. He literally saw red. He couldn't remember another time when he'd been this angry. He wanted to throttle Miranda. The entire time he'd been fighting for their marriage, she'd been looking for the quickest exit out of it.

Grabbing his keys off the hook, he threw open his door and stalked out of his office.

"Are you coming back?" Kindra inquired to his retreating figure.

"No! And hold my calls for the rest of the day!"

Miranda was positive she'd found the best location for Ellicott B & B. She'd been narrowing her choices down between three solid picks. She just hadn't known she was going to use her married name until the art for her logo had come in with both her maiden and married name as options. Jensen B & B or Ellicott B & B. Her married name had won out and Miranda couldn't wait for Vaughn to get home and share the good news with him.

She paused midstride. She wanted to share her news with Vaughn, the man she loved because at the end of the day that was all that mattered. She should have never called her attorney. She didn't really want out of her marriage.

Now that she'd had some time to think about it, Miranda realized the error of her ways.

She was hurt and angry that Vaughn didn't share her same feelings, couldn't repeat them back and she'd wanted to strike out at him. End the marriage. But she would only be hurting herself in the end, because she would be left alone again and this time without Vaughn. Wasn't a life with him, no matter if it was loveless, worth it if they were together? Or maybe she was just fooling herself because she couldn't let him go.

He'd awakened not only her heart, but her body. When they were together, he made her feel completely alive. The need was so strong, so primitive to be joined together as one that Miranda was powerless to deny it. Surely that was better than nothing? Or was she still the weak, spineless woman she'd been in the past? Constantly waiting for a man to love her? Or maybe in time, if given time, love would grow and Vaughn might fall in love with her?

Miranda's thoughts were so muddled that she didn't hear the front door or Vaughn's footsteps until he was standing directly in the dining room doorway.

"Vaughn?" Miranda was scared by his expression. His face was immovable like a stone and a chill ran down her spine.

What on earth could have happened?

"Is everything alright?"

"Perhaps you should tell me." His eyes turned from cold to blazing fury and Miranda started in her chair. Her pulse quickened and her heart began hammering loudly in her chest. "You're the one who's been having secret talks with your attorney. Have you found a way out of your grandfather's clutches so you can end our hasty marriage?"

Miranda gasped and a shiver of panic swept through her. Dear Lord! He'd found out. How could that have happened?

"Nothing to say?" Vaughn inquired. "Because last night, you had plenty to say about love and marriage. And oh wait, trust and respect. But maybe you didn't mean those words for yourself and they were only applicable to me."

"Vaughn...please." Panic was rioting within her.

"Please what? Don't get angry?" His voice began to rise and her stomach clenched tighter. "That you've been lying to me this whole time. I've been completely up front and forthright ever since I revealed my true identity to you. I've never asked you for anything in return except the truth. I guess I just assumed the truth would come with our agreement, but I guess I was wrong."

She shook her head. "You weren't wrong, Vaughn. And I don't know what you think you know, but—"

"What I know is, you've been pretending to enjoy my company, saying you're falling in love with me, all the while you've been secretly planning your escape route," he countered icily.

"That's simply not true."

"Of course it is. I heard from your attorney. He thought he was calling my lawyer, but instead he got me. He filled me in firsthand about the precedent he found. Apparently he felt comfortable talking to me because he thought I wanted to end this farce of a marriage, just like you."

Her spirits sank even lower and Miranda fought to keep the desperation out of her voice. "Our marriage is not a farce. You must believe that—that I love you." She hoped she could reach him by playing the one card she had left in her arsenal, but to her horror, he threw back his head and laughed. He actually laughed and the sound had never sounded uglier.

"Ha! The jig is up, Miranda." His eyes blazed fire at her and his voice was low and taut with anger. "Go ahead and admit that you got what you wanted all along. You got a sucker like me to agree to marry you until I was no longer needed and you could toss me aside. It's no wonder you couldn't wait to get out of my bed. Must have been a real hardship faking all those orgasms."

"Vaughn!" Miranda turned away from him. Her face flushed with humiliation. She didn't want him to see her tears. He'd really cut her to the quick. How could someone she love hurt her so incredibly?

His nostrils flared. "Can't face the truth, huh?"

Miranda spun around and allowed him to see the tears streaming down her cheeks. "I'm not ashamed because I did nothing wrong. I've never faked one moment of our time together, intimate or otherwise. You know that!"

"What I know is that I've been a fool for far too long. I don't want to hear any of your explanations. I just want you out. Now."

"You want me to leave?" she said incredulously. Her words came out tight and twisted because that was exactly how her insides felt. They were a twisted, tangled mess.

"Yes. That's right. I need you to go right now."

"But, Vaughn, we need to talk. You don't understand."

"I understand enough. I know that what I thought was mutual affection and caring was nothing more than a show. You've been looking for a way out this entire time, since our wedding. Do you know how much that hurts?"

Tears blinded her eyes and she choked out, "I'm sorry." Because he was glaring down at her with fathomless eyes like he was her judge, jury and executioner.

"Yes, I'll bet you are," Vaughn sniped. Then he turned on his heel and strode out the door.

"Vaughn, wait, please… .you've got it all wrong." But he was already gone.

Minutes later, she heard the roar of his Ferrari as he sped off and away from the house, away from her.

Miranda stared at the doorway where Vaughn had exited, stunned by the ugliness of his words. How could he think such a thing? Let alone say it? He thought she'd been using him, pretending to fall in love with him? He couldn't be further from the truth. She loved him, more than she'd thought she could.

Miranda was sickened that Vaughn thought she would ever treat him such a manner. She wanted to explain to him that the only reason she'd called her attorney was because she'd run scared just as he was of her feelings for him. She'd thought that by saying those three words aloud that suddenly everything would be magical and made right, but it hadn't been. And so, she'd called her attorney in fear, but as soon as she'd had time to think it over, Miranda had realized what a mistake it was, but now it was too late.

The worst had happened.

It was over.

Vaughn had asked her to leave.

Miranda did the only thing she could. She called her best friend. Thankfully, Sasha answered within seconds of her call. "Hey, girl, how's the married woman doing?"

"Oh, Sasha." Miranda began crying uncontrollably. "I messed up. I really messed up," she sniffed. "I need someplace to stay for a few days."

"Have you and Vaughn had a fight?"

"Yes, no, oh I don't know," Miranda sobbed. "I just know that I can't stay here. Can I please come over?"

"Of course, darling. Are you okay to drive? Do you need me to come pick you up?"

"I'll take a taxi. Just give me a few minutes to throw some things in a suitcase and I'll be there soon."

"Alright. I'll be here for you, girlfriend. Along with a bottle of wine."

Miranda couldn't laugh at Sasha's attempt at a joke because her heart was broken in two. And she doubted it would ever be put back together again.

* * *

Vaughn drove to the beach. It was the one place that usually gave him comfort, but all he could do was stare out at the inky ocean and rail at the moon. So he hopped back in his Ferrari and sped up the coast. He hoped the drive and the speed might clear his head. Instead, he was pulled over by the highway patrol and given a warning to slow down. He was right. Vaughn had no business being on the road, not in his state of mind.

He returned home and found the house empty. Miranda had gone just as he demanded, but it was not what he really wanted. Surely she got that he just needed some space to think? Vaughn wandered through the house feeling like a caged lion with no place to go. He went from to room to room seeking solace, but instead all he found were memories of him and Miranda. The bedroom where they'd made love, the kitchen where they'd made countless meals together and finally out onto the terrace overlooking the pool. His thoughts wandered to the night of the pool party when swimming had turned into an incredible night of passionate lovemaking. Or to the dining room table where Miranda would tap away on her laptop with her hair hanging loose and free without a care in the world. She looked like innocence personified.

But innocent?

No, she was far from it and he felt like howling at the moon.

When he'd come home earlier, she'd looked as if she was happy to see him, but he knew it was all an act. His head was pounding and blood roared in his temples. God, he wanted to shake her. Why didn't she want him as much as he wanted her?

She claimed he had it all wrong, but Vaughn doubted that.

He heard directly from her own attorney and instead of

admitting it, she'd lied to him, thinking he'd be moved by her tears. And usually he was, he'd been raised in a house full of women. He and the Commander were outnumbered, so he hated to see a woman cry. Would do everything in his power to prevent it, but seeing the tears fall from those beautiful brown eyes of hers had hardened his heart.

Damn her.

He should be happy now that she was gone, but instead he felt miserable. Lonely. Incomplete.

Her words of love had almost made him think that he meant something to her other than being the lover that brought out her sensual side. Her sweet, innocent nature had been both maddening and an extremely arousing novelty to him. Miranda was nothing like any of the woman he'd slept with before and it had intrigued him, but more than that, she had made him *feel* things. Things he hadn't wanted or even known he could feel. And he was angry, because now Vaughn wasn't sure if he could ever go back inside his shell again. The shell he'd always had to protect himself. All because he'd begun to care for Miranda.

Maybe, just maybe, even love her.

Chapter 16

After a hot shower, Miranda felt somewhat normal and curled beside Sasha with a cup of tea instead of the wine Sasha had so generously offered when she walked in the door. Apparently, Sasha had said she'd looked so distraught she might need it. And she was. The man Miranda loved had just kicked her out of their home because he thought she had duped him.

"Go ahead, tell me, I told you so," Miranda said, glancing over at Sasha. "I know you want to." She was sure Sasha was going to read her the riot act about getting involved with Vaughn so quickly. And she'd be right. Miranda had fallen headlong, face-first into disaster. When she'd come to San Diego she'd thought she'd had it all figured out. Find a man who was in need of cash and convince him to enter into a marriage of convenience. She never imagined that she would meet a man like Vaughn.

"I'm not going to say any such thing," Sasha responded.

Miranda stared back at her in surprise. "Excuse me?"

"I think you should try to talk to Vaughn, explain things. Help him understand your viewpoint and your fears about giving your heart to another man and getting stomped on again. Right now, Vaughn is angry and when we're angry we're subject to say anything in the heat of the moment."

"Like telling me to get out?"

"I'm sure he didn't mean it."

Miranda's eyes grew large. "Oh, you didn't see him.

There was a storm cloud around him and smoke was billowing from his ears."

"I admit it wasn't Vaughn's finest hour, but cut him some slack. Sounds to me like he's one-hundred percent invested in your relationship and was probably just taken aback that you were still looking for a get-out-of-jail-free card."

"But I wasn't." Miranda shook her head vehemently. "I hadn't so much as thought about Granddaddy's will in weeks. But yesterday, I guess I got scared and made a rash decision that could have cost me my marriage."

Sasha sighed. "Then let's not be rash now. Let the dust settle. And when it does, have an open and honest discussion with the man. I'm sure if you give Vaughn another chance you might be pleasantly surprised what you'll find."

"I don't understand, Sasha. You've been against my marriage since day one. What's changed? Why the change of heart?"

Sasha sighed. "I don't know. I guess I'm as much a romantic as I ever was. And deep down, I think Vaughn might be in love with you too. He just hasn't admitted it to himself. Just like you he could be running scared. You could have the real deal Holyfield."

Miranda couldn't resist a small smile at Sasha's joke. "You really think so? But Vaughn has never said anything. Given me any indication…"

"C'mon, Miranda. Get real," Sasha replied, throwing her hands up in the air. "The man has given you every sign that he's into you. Why else would he have married you?" Before Miranda could get another word in edgewise, Sasha continued, "Listen, you remember how dead set I was against this union?"

"Yes, of course I do. How could I forget?"

"Well, then you don't know this, but I had a serious talk with Vaughn before the ceremony."

Miranda recalled seeing Sasha and Vaughn huddled up. She'd thought Sasha was trying to talk Vaughn *out* of marrying her.

"Vaughn promised me that he liked you and would do right by you. He promised me that he would never hurt you like those other jokers did. And I told him if he did, I was going to punch him in the nose."

"That sounds about right." Miranda snorted and sipped her tea.

"And after our talk, I came to realize that Vaughn just might have fallen in love with you before the wedding. Of course, I don't think he recognized his feelings then, but I was hopeful. If I wasn't, I'm not sure I could have ever let my best friend in the whole wide world go through with marrying a man she hardly knew."

"Alright, so…supposing you're right. What am I supposed to do now?"

"I am right," Sasha stated. "Your challenge will be getting Vaughn to admit he loves you, but if anyone is up for the challenge, it's you, Miranda."

"Have you seen my track record?" She was oh-for-three in the love department.

"I have and because I have, I know that you will fight tooth and nail to get your man back. Trust me, the man's got it bad. Why else would he be so mad? This is a positive sign."

"I hope you're right."

"I'm sorry about yesterday," Vaughn apologized to Kindra late the next morning. He was in no better mood than he was the day before because he'd stayed up half the night thinking about Miranda, but one thing he was sure of was he had no right to take it out on his assistant. She always came through for him no matter the time of day or night and she deserved to be treated much better.

"I appreciate that." Kindra offered him a smile. "I don't know what's going on, but if there's anything I can do to help, you have only to ask."

Vaughn gave her a halfhearted smile. "Thank you. I appreciate that."

"In the meantime, can I tell you that you have a call," Kindra replied. "The private investigator you hired to look into the break-in at Prescott George is on the line."

"Thanks. I'll take the call."

Kindra closed the door behind her because she knew he wanted privacy. He picked up the line.

"Mr. Ellicott, I've uncovered some evidence."

"You have? Is this about the chemical that was found?"

"I think this could have been an inside job."

"I told you that before." Vaughn rubbed his head in exasperation. "So what makes you think so? And who is it, for Christ's sake? Just spit it out."

"Jordan Jace."

"Jordan? That's ridiculous."

"Maybe. Maybe not," the investigator replied. "But the police found residue of a chemical normally used for metalworking which Mr. Jace is known to use in his art."

"That's highly circumstantial," Vaughn replied. "I mean, what possible motive could Jordan have for ransacking the office?" It made no sense. Jordan may not love being a member of Prescott George and usually didn't have time to make every meeting or outing, but Jordan wouldn't sabotage the organization. Or at least Vaughn sure hoped that wasn't the case. "I still need more evidence. I can't go to the members with something this flimsy. I need more. I need you to continue digging."

"As you wish. I just knew you were eager to hear my findings as soon as I had something to report."

"And I am," Vaughn replied. "I just need something more concrete."

"I'm on it."

Vaughn ended the call and stared at the phone incredulously. Jordan vandalizing property? The entire idea was silly. Why the heck was he paying such high fees when the investigator was going to give him far-fetched scenarios? He needed to find something more definitive on who the culprit was before they struck again.

Vaughn leaned back in his chair. He wished he could talk to Miranda about all of this. He'd had overnight to cool off and realized he'd completely overreacted to the news that Miranda had been in contact with her lawyer. He wanted to apologize, to tell her he hadn't meant the awful things he'd said—including that he wanted her out of their home. He just hoped it wasn't too late. He was hoping against hope that after they'd had a chance to sleep on it that she would come home today and they could talk it out. He could convince her that their life together was worth salvaging.

On his way home later that afternoon, Vaughn stopped off at the florist. Because of their falling-out, Vaughn knew that he had to make amends. So he'd called ahead of time to ensure the shop would put together the best flower arrangement Miranda had ever seen because she deserved that much. Lavender roses, Stargazer lilies and dianthus had been artfully arranged and Vaughn couldn't wait to shower her with flowers. Maybe it would smooth things over and get things to return to the way they were. He also wanted to know Miranda's thoughts on the entire break-in situation. She'd met Jordan. What would she think about the investigator's comments?

The house however was empty when he arrived. Maybe she was upstairs? Flowers in hand, he ran up the stairs to her room. He hadn't had the heart to walk past her room last night because he hadn't wanted to see there, but he did now. It would be where Miranda would go if she needed distance from him. He stopped at the doorway of her room and his heart tightened in his chest at the sight that greeted him. Her bed was untouched. The doors to the walk-in closet were wide open. Slowly he walked toward it, already knowing what he'd find.

It was empty. All of Miranda's things were gone.

She'd left him.

Crushed, Vaughn sank to the floor and tossed the flowers aside. Why had he been so hard on her? Why had he told her to leave? If he'd just asked her calmly why she was contacting her attorney instead of flying off the rails, he wouldn't be in this position now. Alone. Without his woman. Vaughn fingered his ring.

Was it really over between them?

That was when Vaughn saw the note lying on her bed. Grabbing it, Vaughn scanned the contents. Miranda apologized for getting him into the marriage. She expressed that she should have never come to San Diego, but she wasn't sorry she had. She said she loved him and wished him the best in life, even if it wasn't with her.

Did she honestly think he'd have a life without her in it?

He pulled his phone out of his jacket and dialed her number. It went straight to voice mail. He dialed it again and got the same result. She was probably declining his calls on the other end.

That was when it struck him what he'd been trying so hard not to face. The new emotion surged in him like adrenaline. Somehow the core of ice that had existed within him, a place he hadn't known existed, had thawed when Miranda had come into his life.

He loved her.

Maybe he always had, but because he'd never seen what love looked like, because his parents had a cold marriage, he hadn't known what it was. He'd spent much of the last decade on a ship protecting his country because all he'd ever known was duty, honor and sacrifice. Values that had been ingrained in him by the Commander. The only time he'd spent with women was when his anatomy required it.

And since then, he'd been running, spending much of his life traveling and burying himself in his work or in the waves and shutting himself off, not letting anyone close. But then Miranda came along and suddenly things were different. The more he'd tried to relegate his feelings for her as lust, the more she'd quietly come in and stolen his heart. As the weeks had gone by, he'd grown to love having her in his life. She was in him, a part of him and what he felt for her was more powerful than anything he'd ever experienced in his life.

And it terrified him. Maybe that was why he'd felt possessive over her, like when he'd seen her getting chummy with Jordan. He'd known Miranda would never cheat on him, but the fear nonetheless had been irrational. Miranda was his. And only his.

But he'd treated her abominably. The pain and hurt on her face yesterday when he'd railed at her had grabbed at his chest. He didn't deserve her and probably never did, but that didn't mean he wouldn't try to salvage what they had. Miranda was everything he could ever hope for. Beautiful. Smart. Sexy. Perfect in every way and Vaughn hated to think he'd damaged her, made her doubt herself again. Not when he'd spent much of the last few weeks building up her self-confidence. She'd emerged as a self-confident lady who maybe didn't love him anymore.

He shook his head. No. He wouldn't let it happen. He couldn't lose her. He needed her. Loved her.

And he knew what he had to do.

Ring. Ring. The buzz of the phone interrupted his self-analysis. "Hello." Anxious to get to Miranda, he answered gruffly. It was one of his salesmen, pleading with him to take a look at a prospectus that was due that evening.

Reluctantly, Vaughn rushed out of the room to his office to pitch open one of his many laptops. He was scrolling through his emails when a name popped out at him.

Sasha Charles. He quickly scanned the message. She was ready to have his head if he hurt Miranda, but he had one shot at getting it right.

He would have to get with his salesman tomorrow. He had more important things to do. And that was getting Miranda back.

"When are you going to talk to Vaughn?" Sasha inquired as she and Miranda took a stroll along the La Jolla Shores beach. Since she'd married Vaughn, this beach was one of Miranda's favorite places. She could see why Vaughn came here when he needed to clear his mind.

"Soon."

"Why are you avoiding seeing him?"

Miranda kept walking and didn't answer. She knew why. She was afraid to confront him. Was afraid he would hurt her again and she couldn't bear it if he did. If she went to him a second time and laid her heart bare and he turned his back on her, Miranda didn't know what she would do.

"Answer me, woman," Sasha said, spinning her around.

Miranda looked up at her best friend with tears in her eyes. And without her having to say a word, Sasha enveloped her in a hug. "Shh. Shh." She tried to quiet Miranda's sobs, but now that the dam had been broken, there was no place for Miranda to hide. She would have to face her fears head-on. She fell to her knees in the sand and Sasha joined her.

When she could finally find her voice, she said, "You've no idea how hard it was for me when Jake left me. It hurt so bad I physically ached inside." Vaughn was the one man who could take her back to that horribly lonely place where she'd been on the brink of devastation. Before, she'd barely had the strength to build her world from ground zero. Miranda wasn't sure she could do it all over again. "I don't want to go back there, Sasha. I refuse to. I'm a much stronger woman than I was back then."

"And I don't want you to. You are strong and it's because I've seen this change in you, this quiet strength that I'm asking you to take a risk again."

"That's easy for you to say, Sasha. You haven't been where I've been."

"True, but when I see you hurting like this and knowing there might be a solution if only you're willing to be brave. Well, it kind of makes me sad, Miranda. You see, you and Vaughn were making me believe in love at first sight."

"Aaaw." Fresh tears sprang to Miranda's eyes and Sasha leaned across the sand to hug her. "It's going to be okay, Miranda. I believe that with all my heart."

"How?" Miranda asked. "How can you say that? Look at where I am now."

Sasha smiled broadly and Miranda couldn't on earth think of why. Then she turned to follow the direction of Sasha's gaze and saw why.

Vaughn.

He was walking straight toward them in the sand, wearing a business suit. It looked like he'd come directly from work. Instead of his usual beach getup of shorts and a tank underneath his wet suit. What felt like joy began to bubble inside her, but Miranda pushed it down. She couldn't get her hopes up, only to have them dashed. What was he doing here? And how did he know where they were going to be?

Miranda turned to Sasha and saw the smug smile on her face.

That little matchmaker!

"You did this, didn't you?" Miranda pointed a finger in her best friend's direction.

Sasha shrugged her shoulders and then rose to her feet, brushing off the sand. "You needed a little shove in the right direction, so I thought I might help you along. Vaughn." She nodded to Miranda's husband when he stopped several feet away from them.

Miranda peered up at him with her hand shielding the sun. "What do you want?"

"We need to talk."

"And that's my cue to make my exit, but I'm not going far," Sasha said, pointing her finger at Vaughn. "Don't make me regret tossing you a bone," Miranda heard her whisper. Then her friend was stepping several yards away.

When Vaughn saw Miranda's figure next to Sasha's, the pain in his chest eased somewhat. They may be estranged, but he hadn't lost her yet. She was still here in San Diego and he could still reach her, get through to her, if he was willing to be vulnerable and tell Miranda his true feelings. Feelings he had only just discovered once she'd left and he'd thought she was gone forever.

"Can I sit beside you?" he asked, staring down into her angelic face. Her eyes were puffy and bloodshot red. He could see that she'd been crying and he hated that he was the cause, but he never would be again. At least not intentionally. He didn't wait for her response. Instead, he sat beside Miranda. His body hummed with awareness of having her near. He glanced in her direction.

His wife. His love.

It staggered him that he'd just come to the realization that he loved her, was in love with Miranda.

"Your suit."

He shrugged. "I don't care about the darn suit. I came here for you, Miranda."

"Don't say things you don't mean, Vaughn, because you think that's what I want to hear. We don't want the same things. Love. Marriage. A partnership. Children. Can you honestly tell me you want those things?" Tears glistened in her eyes as she spoke.

He stared back at her. "Yes, yes I do. Very much so."

Miranda shook her head as if she didn't believe him. "Then you're fooling yourself," she said, rising to her feet. "You were only looking for a temporary wife, not the whole lot."

"Well, I'm telling you I've changed my mind." He followed behind her as she trudged through the sand, uncaring of the designer shoes on his feet.

"Why?"

"Because of you."

"Me?" A perplexed expression came across her face and she stopped walking. "I don't understand. I thought you weren't looking for a deeper relationship?"

"I wasn't," Vaughn responded. "Not until I came home today and saw that you'd left me for good. I thought we'd had just an argument, a bad one, but an argument nonetheless. And I came home, expecting to find you there to share the news about my day and the break-in, but you weren't there. And when I went to your room and saw your empty closet, I thought you'd gone and were never coming back."

"I had gone," Miranda said. "Or at least I thought I was."

Hope filled Vaughn at her words. "Was? Does that mean you've had a change of heart?"

Miranda sighed. "I admit that I was going to come back and talk to you."

"So I haven't lost you?"

"Do you want to?" Her beautiful brown eyes peered up at him and he knew he'd made the right choice coming here today.

"No, I don't want to lose you, Miranda. You were right last night. When you called me out on my fears. Because

I was scared. Am scared. You see, I'm deathly afraid of loving you and being loved by you. Men in my family were always taught that emotion was a sign of weakness. So I've never truly seen what love looks like, feels like and so when I felt these strange emotions, I chalked it up to lust and the undeniable chemistry between us. But that wasn't all."

"There's more? Cause you're off to a really good start and I wouldn't want you to ruin it with too much talk."

Vaughn chuckled. That was his Miranda, constantly surprisingly him and keeping him off-kilter. "I'm sorry, truly sorry for everything I said last night. I was running scared and I hurt you and for that I'm sorry. Since you've come into my life, you've made me feel more alive than I have ever felt. I'd been surfing through my life from one endless wave and business deal and from one temporary relationship to another, instead of living it. But I don't want to do that anymore. I don't want to be like my father, I want to feel things. I want to be loved."

She laughed and tears spilled down her cheek. "Oh, Vaughn." She leaned over and stroked his cheek.

"I can't believe I've lived my entire life without experiencing what true love really is. I'm so thankful I saw you sitting on this very beach a month ago."

"Does that mean…?"

"Yes. It means I love you, Miranda. I think I've loved you from the very start."

"He did," Sasha piped in from several yards away where she had been surprisingly quiet. "I could see it in his eyes. Once I met him and talked to him, I just knew it."

"Thanks for the assist, Sasha," Vaughn said, "but I've got it from here." He took Miranda's hands in his. "Being with you has taught me what love means and I never want to live a day without you. Last night, not having you beside me was hell on earth. I want to wake up every morning and see your smiling face beside mine."

"You do?"

A hoarse chuckle escaped his lips. "Oh yes, I love you, Miranda." He hauled her into his arms. "Can you still love me too even after I hurt you?"

"If you ever hurt me again…"

"I won't. I want to spend the rest of my life with you and I promise to love and cherish you and to never hurt you again." Vaughn pulled away long enough to lower himself to the ground and on one knee asked, "Will you marry me?"

"We're already married," she said, laughing.

"I know we're already married, but I'd like us to renew our vows, because this time we mean them." He gathered her in his arms into a whirlpool of a kiss that sent her heart soaring and made her blood race. His lips both demanded and caressed hers with equal intensity.

"Ahem, ahem." There was coughing behind him and Vaughn realized Sasha was still standing nearby. Slowly, he lifted his head. Glancing down at Miranda he saw she was just as dazed as he was by that kiss. They needed to move this to a more private location where it was just the two of them. Because one thing was for certain: he didn't want to go another night like the last one without her taste on his lips before he went to sleep.

"Sasha, I can't thank you enough for telling me where to find Miranda. We just might have to name our firstborn after you."

"Ha, ha, ha." Sasha chuckled. "But it was my pleasure. I knew you two were meant to be after our talk before your marriage ceremony. Now if you'll excuse me, my work here is done." With a squeeze of Miranda's shoulders, Sasha was walking through the sand back to her car.

"About that firstborn comment," Miranda said, and

raised an eyebrow. "Are you thinking about babies already?"

"Only if you want them," Vaughn responded.

Miranda smiled right back at him. "And only if they're yours."

Epilogue

"I didn't think it was possible to be this happy," Vaughn said a few days later.

After they'd professed their love to each on the beach, they'd returned to their home in La Jolla and had made up for lost time. They hadn't left their house in days and instead had been enjoying each other and having a very private honeymoon. Vaughn wrapped his arm around his wife because moments ago, she had come out on the balcony wearing the sexy peignoir he'd bought for her. When she'd first walked out in the moonlight wearing the divine, sheer concoction of silk that left little to the imagination, he'd openly stared at her. He could see her long legs underneath. See the dusky hue of her nipples across the top of the lace which showed him plenty of cleavage. He licked his lips in anticipation of another evening of lovemaking.

"Neither did I," Miranda said. "I thought I was always going to be unlucky in love."

"Not anymore," Vaughn said. "I will always be by your side. No matter where we are. Speaking of, we haven't yet discussed where our home base is going to be."

Miranda turned around to stare at him. "I guess I just assumed it would always be here. This is Elite's headquarters."

"True." Vaughn nodded. "But it's not a foregone conclusion. I don't expect you to uproot yourself permanently. You have family, you have friends in the Windy City. If you really want to go back home, I could learn to put up with the Chicago winters."

"You would do that for me?"

"I would do anything for you, Miranda. You're the love of my life."

Miranda had waited her entire life to hear those words and they had never sounded as sweet as they did coming from her husband. The man she'd come to crave, adore and love in every way imaginable. If anyone had told her when she'd come to San Diego a month ago on a husband hunt that she would find the man she was meant to spend the rest of her days with, she would have told them they were a fool.

But it happened.

It happened to her.

And she was no longer embarrassed by the pure admiration and lust lurking in those dark depths when he looked at her. Instead it made her hot with longing and ratcheted up the sexual tension sizzling between them whenever they were within a few feet of each other.

"I kind of like California," Miranda said. "And with Elite's headquarters here and my luxury bed-and-breakfast by the ocean in Malibu, it's the perfect fit. Plus, I wouldn't dream of making a California boy like you brave the Midwest winters. So the worst you'll have to contend with is I-5 traffic."

"I-5 traffic?" Vaughn chuckled. "Why drive when I can take a private jet?"

Miranda laughed as she locked her arms around his neck and brushed her lips against his. "That's why I love you, Vaughn, because with you I'll never get bored. With you, I've found my forever home."

* * * * *

COMING NEXT MONTH
Available March 20, 2018

#565 STILL LOVING YOU
The Grays of Los Angeles • by Sheryl Lister
Malcolm Gray is Lauren Emerson's biggest regret. Eight years ago, a lack of trust cost her a future with the star running back. Now an opportunity brings the nutrition entrepreneur home, where she hopes to declare a truce. But their first encounter unleashes explosive passion. Is this their second chance?

#566 SEDUCED IN SAN DIEGO
Millionaire Moguls • by Reese Ryan
There's nothing conventional about artist Jordan Jace, except his membership to the exclusive Millionaire Moguls. And when he meets marketing consultant Sasha Charles, persuading the straitlaced beauty to break some rules is an irresistible challenge. But their affair may be temporary, unless they can discover the art of love—together…

#567 ONE UNFORGETTABLE KISS
The Taylors of Temptation • by A.C. Arthur
All navy pilot Garrek Taylor ever wanted was to fly far from his family's past. But with his wings temporarily clipped, he's back in his hometown. His plans are sidetracked when he wins a date with unconventional house restorer Harper Presley. Will their combustible connection lead to an everlasting future?

#568 A BILLIONAIRE AFFAIR
Passion Grove • by Niobia Bryant
Alessandra Dalmount has been groomed to assume the joint reins of her father's empire. Now that day has arrived, forcing her to work closely with co-CEO and childhood nemesis Alek Ansah. As they battle for control of the billion-dollar conglomerate, can they turn their rivalry into an alliance of love?

Get 2 Free Books,
Plus 2 Free Gifts—
just for trying the
Reader Service!

K I M A N I™ ROMANCE

SPECIAL EXCERPT FROM

HARLEQUIN

*Malcolm Gray is Lauren Emerson's biggest regret. Eight years
ago, a lack of trust cost her a future with the star running
back. Now an opportunity brings the nutrition entrepreneur
home, where she hopes to declare a truce. But their first
encounter unleashes explosive passion...and unwanted
memories of the precious dreams they once shared. As they
jockey for position, a new set of rules could change the game
for both of them...*

Read on for a sneak peek at
STILL LOVING YOU,
the next exciting installment in the
THE GRAYS OF LOS ANGELES *series by Sheryl Lister!*

Mr. Green stood, helped her with her chair and waved at someone. "I know you're still meeting with players, but have you
had a chance to meet Malcolm Gray yet?"

The hairs stood up on the back of her neck. Before she could
respond, she felt the heat and, without turning around, knew it
was Malcolm.

"Congratulations, Malcolm," Mr. Green said, shaking
Malcolm's hand. "Have you met Lauren Emerson? She's going
to be a great asset to the team."

Malcolm stared down into Lauren's eyes. "Thanks, and yes,
we've met. Hello, Lauren."

That's one way to describe it. "Hi, Malcolm." She had only
seen photos of him wearing a tuxedo, and those pictures hadn't
come close to capturing the raw magnetism he exuded standing
next to her. She couldn't decide whether she liked him better

with his locs or the close-cropped look he now sported.

"Well, my wife is going to have my head if we don't get at least one dance in, so I'll see you two later. Malcolm, can you make sure Lauren gets acquainted with everyone?"

Lauren's eyes widened. "Oh, I'll be fine. I'm sure Malcolm has some other people to see." She looked to Malcolm, expecting him to agree. To her amazement, he extended his arm.

"Shall we?"

With Mr. Green and his wife staring at her with huge smiles, she couldn't very well say what she wanted. Instead, she took his arm and let him lead her out to the dance floor. She regretted it the moment he wrapped his arm around her. Malcolm kept a respectable distance, but it didn't matter. His closeness caused an involuntary shiver to pass through her. And why did he have to smell so good? The fragrance had a perfect balance of citrus and earth that was as comforting as it was sensual. How was she going to make it through the next five minutes?

Malcolm must have sensed her nervousness. "Relax, Lauren. We've danced closer than this, so what's the problem?"

Lauren didn't need any reminders of how close they'd been in the past. "I'm fine," she mumbled.

A minute went by and Malcolm said, "Smile. You don't want everyone to think you're not enjoying my company."

She glared up at him. "You're enjoying this, aren't you?"

He grinned. "I'm holding a beautiful woman in my arms. What's not to enjoy?"

Mr. Green and his wife smiled Lauren's way, and she smiled back. As soon as they turned away, she dropped her smile. "I can't play these games with you, Malcolm," she whispered harshly.

"This is no game." Their eyes locked for a lengthy moment, then he pulled her closer and kept up the slow sway.

Don't miss STILL LOVING YOU by Sheryl Lister, available April 2018 wherever Harlequin® Kimani Romance™ books and ebooks are sold.

Want to give in to temptation with
steamy tales of irresistible desire?

Check out **Harlequin® Presents®,
Harlequin® Desire** and
Harlequin® Kimani™ Romance books!

New books available every month!

CONNECT WITH US AT:

Harlequin.com/Community

 Facebook.com/HarlequinBooks

Twitter.com/HarlequinBooks

Instagram.com/HarlequinBooks

Pinterest.com/HarlequinBooks

ReaderService.com

**ROMANCE WHEN
YOU NEED IT**

PGENRE2017

LOVE
Harlequin
romance?

Join our Harlequin community to share your thoughts and connect with other romance readers!

Be the first to find out about promotions, news, and exclusive content!

Sign up for the Harlequin e-newsletter and download a free book from any series at

www.TryHarlequin.com

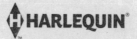